THE RESURRECTION OF LADY SOMERSET
may just be the death of the Jonathan Rexley.

mon ... nd the ...awell, ... med to
float across the room, her white muslin ... flowing
around her, caressing her legs as a cool breeze touches
the cheek on a hot summer's day. Her hair, adorned with
a ring of fresh flowers, shone the colour of the sun at its
hottest white, her skin the palest alabaster.

No wonder she had been redubbed the Somerset
Ghost. She was otherworldly. But *angel* would have been
a more appropriate moniker. She was beautiful, not
frightening. Drinking in the sight of her awakened
feelings he didn't know he had—chivalrous, protective
desires...and something more base, more passionate. The
yen to reach out, lift her into his arms, and carry her off
to private a rendezvous began to melt his anger, and he
immediately knew he needed to be wary of this
bewitching creature.

He stiffened his spine and schooled his countenance.
"You have been hiding in the shadows like a rat, Miss
Blackwell. What say you of this? Did you know of my
father's plans to saddle us together? Did you have act in
them?"

As he fired questions at her, she shook her head
adamantly, her face strained with evident worry. He
ignored it, refusing to be swayed by feminine wiles.

"Why do you not speak, vixen? Do you not realize you
will never prevail? Answer my queries." He quieted for a
moment and studied her teary-eyed mien.

She looked like a chastised child, and for a moment,
he felt a twinge of guilt at crucifying her. He opened his
mouth to speak, but Smythe touched his arm, drew his
attention. He scarcely had time to comprehend what was
happening before Lark picked up her skirt and fled the
room.

The Resurrection of Lady Somerset

By

Nicola Beaumont

The Resurrection of Lady Somerset

COPYRIGHT © 2007 by Nicola T. Martinez

Cover Art by *Tamra Westberry*

The Wild Rose Press
PO Box 706
Adams Basin, NY 14410-0706
Visit us at www.thewildrosepress.com

Publishing History
First Line English Tea Rose Edition, September 2007
PRINT ISBN 1-60154-066-3

Published in the United States of America

Dedication

To J.C., my heart. Thanks for always holding my hand.
Without You, I have nothing;
with You, I have my heart's desire.

Chapter One

Lark Blackwell sat unobserved as Chauncy, the butler, escorted the family members one by one into the library. The dim sconce and fire light flicked shadows across the leather-spined books lining the walls, but did not illuminate her darkened corner. She was glad of that fact. The thought of being around people after so many years of seclusion scared her to death.

The first to arrive was Harriet, Lady Wescotte of Chiswick. She flounced into the library on a dash of cold air and pushed her rather large bottom onto a gilt-edged chair with as much aplomb as a person of her girth could muster. Behind her trailed a young gentleman of an age not more than ten-and-four. His emaciated legs bobbled underneath him as he tried to make haste. They made an odd pair, Lark thought delightedly. Perhaps not having to hide any longer would prove to be more exciting than she had anticipated. She smiled to herself as she pressed her back into the chair, content to sit and watch her extended family for a little while longer before revealing her presence.

"Here, Mama, let me hold your things for you." The young lad scampered to Lady Wescotte's side and tried to remove a set of papers from her chubby, ring-endowed fingers.

The older woman snatched her hand from his grasp and swatted at his fingers. "Widgeon! As if I would entrust you to such weighty documents. These are your future, boy, and since you are so dim-witted, I trust it's the only future you are likely to get."

The lad's dark head drooped as he silently made a place for himself beside the chair his mother had chosen. A pang of compassion pierced Lark's heart. How harsh the woman was. And the poor boy, he seemed utterly crushed. Lark began to have second thoughts about

1

revealing herself. She wasn't equipped to spar with such a viperous tongue.

When next Chauncy slid open the carved mahogany doors, he graciously announced to Lady Wescotte the arrival of Cyril Rexley. Rexley wore a staid expression. His jaw was set in hard angles, and his aquiline nose came to a sharp edge at the tip, yet there was nothing harsh in his dark eyes. He bowed politely to Lady Wescotte. "Pleasure to see you again, Aunt Harriet. And you, too, my dear young Geoffry," he added as though it were an afterthought.

Lark's heart silently screamed for the boy. Did everyone treat poor Geoffry as a burden? There seemed to be nothing wrong with him. Good gracious, if they rejected *him* for no apparent reason, what would they do to *her* when they discovered her deficiency?

A sudden chill tingled through her—little pins and needles of foreboding. This was all a terrible mistake. Regardless of being invited, she shouldn't have come. She should have stayed in her suites and devised her own plan for the rest of her life—escaped Somerset Manor before anyone discovered her. But Lord Peter had seemed so positive, so enthusiastic.

Oh, why had she believed him?

She knew why. She'd believed him, because she'd wanted to. She wanted the life he offered.

Lady Wescotte waved away Cyril's remark with a pudgy hand. "Oh, don't waste your niceties on me, Cyril Rexley. We have a passion for hating one another, and I would rather share an honest antipathy than a cordial acquaintance with the likes of you. You are a wastrel. Everybody knows it. Your dear departed father," she bowed her head reverently, "my brother, rest his soul, knew it, too. If he has left you anything at all, it is probably only your right to go to debtor's prison." She glanced at the floor, draping her face with sympathy. "God knows what would have happened had you been the eldest son."

Lark didn't have much experience with people, but she didn't believe for one minute, the look of sorrow on Lady Wescotte's face was sincere.

"So you think Papa would disengage his own son in

favor of yours, I take it?" Cyril, seemingly unaffected by Lady Wescotte's disparagement, looked at the woman with an amusement in his eyes. Giving a practiced flip to the tail of his coat, he seated himself on a settee near the fireplace. "Jonathon is soon to be named the new Lord Somerset. What makes you think your son will inherit anything of value?" Cyril crossed one leg over the other and turned to Geoffry. "Sorry, chum, but it is the truth. Not exactly top of the crop, are you?"

Geoffry shifted his feet nervously and looked to his overbearing mother for support. His silent plea went untended as Lady Wescotte ignored her son and leveled her fierce retort at Cyril. "What I have in store for my son is nothing to do with you. My business is with Lord Somerset."

"Ah, well in that case, *Lady Wescotte*, I shall leave you to it then," he replied with indignant formality. "Wouldn't want to poke my nose in where it's not wanted and get it tweaked off now, would I?"

Lark wanted to chuckle at Cyril's banter with his aunt. He certainly displayed the rogue's wit and tongue Lark had read about in books. His openness appealed to her, and she wondered if Jonathon Rexley would prove to be as honest. She hoped so. She tried to conjure his image from the recesses of her childhood memories but could not envision anything that would tell her if he were a gentleman or a rogue.

Light streamed in from the great room as Chauncy escorted in yet another relative. Lark inhaled a quick, silent breath. Jonathon Rexley, the new Lord Somerset, stood with commanding presence on the threshold of the library. His dark coat and breeches defined his masculine form and the sight of him blanketed her with warmth. An impeccably tied cravat shimmered around his neck even in the dim light.

He resembled his brother—the rigid shape of their faces matched—yet Lord Somerset's countenance seemed more stern and serious. His dark eyes scanned the room, and he smiled politely at his kinsmen.

"Show Mr. Smythe in the minute he arrives, Chauncy. We shall have this awful business over and done as quickly as possible." Jonathon turned to face the butler.

"Yes, my lord." Chauncy bowed out of the room, sliding the library doors closed behind him.

Jonathon made his way to Lady Wescotte. "Aunt Harriet." He bowed slightly. "I certainly wish we were come together in better circumstances."

"I, too, Jonathon. Your father was a good man. A trifle too good, at times," she added as if she could not extend the compliment without, too, attaching a criticism.

Jonathon smiled wanly. "One can never be too good, Aunt Harriet." He turned his attention to Geoffry.

Lord Somerset held out a hand and took the boy's reluctant one. "And you, you have grown no less than a foot since last we saw one another. Why, you are practically a man now." Jonathon shook the lad's hand vigorously, evidently ignoring the faltering look Geoffry returned him. Lord Somerset gave the boy a reassuring smile and released his grip.

Nearing the fireplace, Jonathon turned his attention to his younger brother. "Still a regular at the clubs, I take it?"

"It has been less than a fortnight since you traveled to Leicester, surely you cannot expect I would turn about that quickly?" Cyril's brows rose in amusement.

Jonathon sighed. "One can but hope, Cyril."

He gave his brother a reproachful glance that made Lark wonder what thoughts traveled through Jonathon's mind. A mixture of weariness and disappointment marred his handsome face, and she felt the odd urge to comfort him. Strange that he would draw her so, since she hadn't seen him in years.

"So how does it feel being back in the old lair?" Cyril asked, ignoring Jonathon's reproof.

"This is our home, Cyril, why do you insist on this constant cynicism?" Jonathon's gaze locked with his brother's in a challenge Lark remembered.

"You must admit, it's not as if the old codger welcomed us back here with open arms. He practically turned us out at majority then bolted the door behind us. How often do you suppose a father refuses to see his children without appointment? Downright odd is what the man was."

Jonathon's mouth set in a thin line. He started to speak but turned in silence to the blazing fire instead. The lapping flames captured his attention for a short time before he looked up to the portrait of his mother over the mantle. Again, his eyes became clouded with something Lark could not grasp but wished to understand.

She studied him intently, wanting to mark indelibly to memory his every curve and expression. She had dreamed of him for so long, it hardly seemed real that he was now standing in front of her. At this moment, he looked so helpless, like the time when he'd been ill and she'd made her way into his bedchamber to watch him sleep. His slumber, then, had been blemished by fever and distress. Now, with his countenance so marked with sadness, Lark wanted nothing more than to place a soothing caress across his cheek, just as she had then.

****

Sadness swept over Jonathon. More than a decade had past since his mother had been trapped in the fire that claimed her life and the lives and home of her dearest friends with her. Now his father was gone, too. He suddenly felt completely alone in the world. Cyril was more a burden than a brother, wasting his life at White's and Tatt's, leading the life of a rake with no responsibility. Such as it was for the second son who had no estate obligation.

Behind him sat Aunt Harriet, a vulture waiting for her meal to die in some faraway Arabian desert. He had never liked her much. A kind word rarely passed her lips. She was a harpy, but he would continue to tolerate her because she was his father's sister—and Peter Rexley had always insisted on tolerance.

Cyril was right about the strange behavior their father had embraced. But Jonathon had long since come to terms with that oddity and now could not blame the man for wanting to turn away from the harsh world that had consumed his only love.

Affairs of the heart were much too risky to one's sanity. There were plenty of women to accommodate a man's sensitivities who did not require the emotional attachment that had caused his father's odd reclusiveness.

Besides, Peter Rexley had not been *that* standoffish with his sons. Jonathon distinctly remembered a time not five years past when he had been quite out of curl, and his father had sent Chauncy along to fetch him home. A man without his head wouldn't have done that.

It was then that Jonathon had come face to face with the Somerset ghost. Of course, he didn't really believe in ghosts. Only nodcocks and women did. And he had been out of his mind with fever. Still, he remembered a beautiful figure leaning over him, caressing his forehead with soft fingers. Her skin appeared as snow white as the gown she wore, her hair hanging about her cheeks so long that it almost touched his face.

"Who are you," he'd croaked through a parched throat, reaching out to her. She felt like satin. He wanted her to whisk him away—away from the fever and from the discomfort of life in the shadow of his father's strange behavior.

She smiled and her eyes softened in a way that would be in his memory forever. But she did not reply, only pressed a slender finger to her lips and then to his own. He had blinked, and she was gone.

Jonathon shook his head and dissolved his musings, then turned to face his remaining family. He needed to keep his mind on the present and not stuff it with feathery reflections that did no one any good.

"Smythe should arrive shortly and we shall have this nasty legal business over with," he told them. "Has anyone heard from Marie?"

"My daughter has seen fit to cavort with the likes of a mere landowner. He possesses no title and no breadth of knowledge regarding the proper etiquette of the *ton*—he tends to his own land, *physically*, I assure you." Lady Wescotte's hefty jowls wrinkled in disgust. "I have no use for that girl now. She has taken my careful training and my advice and tossed it into my face as if I were some common, ignorant fishwife."

"She married the gentleman, Aunt Harriet. You make it sound as if Marie took leave of her senses and became a fallen woman."

"Humph," Lady Wescotte replied, as if the grumble was a sufficient answer.

"I take that to mean you have not heard from Marie," Jonathon surmised. He turned a questioning gaze to Cyril.

Cyril chuckled. "Haven't set eyes on a respectable woman in more days than I can count. Are you positive the missive reached her?"

Before Jonathon could answer, the library doors opened once more. Chauncy escorted in the Honorable Bentley Smythe, the Rexley family's solicitor. Smythe's balding head seemed determined to be a magnet for the room's dim yellow light, and as he approached, he appeared to be adorned by a golden halo.

Smythe's lack of hair was a source of great amusement for Cyril, and knowing his brother well, Jonathon flung the younger man a warning glance that only proved to widen the grin on Cyril's face.

"Evening everyone," Smythe said, glancing over all the Rexley relatives in the room. He took a moment to bow politely to Lady Wescotte. "My lady, a pleasure to see you again after so many years."

"The luxury belongs to me, Mr. Smythe, I assure you," Lady Wescotte replied flatly. She turned slightly, motioning to the young lad beside her. "You remember my son, Geoffry?"

For a moment Mr. Smythe's face whitened, his entire lanky frame stiffening. Regaining his composure, he smiled kindly at Geoffry. "You were but a babe in your mother's arms the last time I saw you. You have certainly grown into an admirable specimen."

As he was inclined to do, Geoffry quavered for a response. His hesitation was rewarded by a commotion intruding the library from the great room.

"La, Chauncy, there is no time for formality. I am ages in arrears as it is." The library doors flew open and Marie Beauchamps entered the room with the most unladylike haste. Chauncy skipped steps behind her, catching the lady's pelisse and bonnet as she tossed them at him carelessly. Her golden ringlets bobbed around her face, giving her a girlish mien as she bounced into the room. She immediately approached Jonathon, embracing him warmly. "Dear Cousin, it is so good to see you again." Her expression sobered and she showed him a grave look.

"Such a tragedy is this that Uncle Peter should be gone aloft."

He patted his cousin affectionately on the arm and extended her a warm smile. "'Tis but the will of God that this sorrow brings you into this home again, Cousin. You are a fresh breeze in these stagnant halls. You've stayed away from us far too long."

"You are right, indeed, but my country home keeps me quite busy." A sparkle leapt into her blue eyes. "And my husband as well. He shall be wanting heirs soon, I fear."

At the sound of Lady Wescotte's grumble, Marie turned to face her mother. "Apparently absence has not caused your heart to grow fonder of my marriage?"

"You were the belle of the Season during your come-out, Marie. Could've had your pick of any number residing in Regent's Square, yet you chose this...this *landowner* with no title." The manner in which Lady Wescotte spat the word, one would have thought 'landowner' to be a vile profanity.

"I love him, Mama," Marie said on a whisper.

"Utter nonsense. Love has addled your brain." Lady Wescotte shook her head and waved away her daughter with both hands. "You wed the man, and I wash my hands of you. You made your bed and now you must lie in it. You will get no help from me when your fingers bleed from working. Heavens, you don't even have an abigail. No doubt you actually traveled here unattended."

"I assure you, I have no regrets." She smiled at Jonathon and bestowed a wink on him. "Save perhaps, that Jonathon here decided upon bachelorhood too long."

Lady Wescotte shot a scathing look in Cyril's direction. "Well, you could have chosen worse, I suppose," she conceded, although, coming from _her_ lips the words did not sound like much of a concession.

"Unfortunately, the same could not be said of poor Beauchamps. Look at the family he got gummed up with," Cyril mumbled.

Jonathon dispensed a scathing look to his brother and Bentley Smythe took the opportunity to call the gathering to order.

Lady Wescotte opened her mouth to utter something,

but deferred to Smythe's timely call.

"It is a tragic time for the Rexley family," the solicitor began.

Jonathon stood with his back as straight as a rail and held a stony expression on his face. It would do him no good to show emotion now.

"But, as you all know, Peter Rexley, Lord Somerset, had not been himself for quite sometime," Smythe went on. "Many had thought his mind to be gone, although I did not share in this belief. He had become a hardened recluse in the decade prior to his calling aloft, but as his body began to fail him I was called forth as family friend and solicitor to administrate his bidding and thus I will do so now."

A blanket of sorrow descended upon the room and silence reigned. Even Lady Wescotte sat in deference to the passing of her brother—although only for a moment. Then she shifted in her chair and the papers in her hand rustled. Jonathon thought the noise distastefully amplified in the joyless calm and he knew a moment of unease as he watched her face settle into a smug guise.

Marie drew his attention as she took a seat in the armchair nearest her mother. She smiled kindly at her younger brother.

Jonathon remained standing, knowing that if he tried anything as inert as sitting he would probably end up in Bedlam.

His father had been the only person in his family—indeed, in his life—with whom he had ever felt a rapport. After the older man turned out his sons, Jonathon strove to remove all emotion from his life, and had succeeded rather well.

As he glanced at the menagerie of people in the room, the new Lord Somerset decided that his lack of family ties was more a blessing than not. Marie was the only one of merit in the lot. He admired her for standing up to her mother's tirades and marrying the man that she, herself, had chosen. Jonathon had spent much of his salad days waffling between trying to fit in and not caring at all for the approval of the *ton*. He had finally concluded that there was far too much work involved in pleasing everyone but had gained a respectability that afforded him a little more freedom to do what he chose.

Cyril, on the other hand, had chosen to do his own will without the benefit of gaining respectability. He was a thorn in Jonathon's side, brother or not, and it grated on his nerves to know that his brother was such a wastrel. It was an undeniable blessing that Jonathon had been born the elder son, for only God Himself knew what would happen to the estate were Cyril to get his hands on it.

Jonathon turned his attention back to Bentley Smythe with the fleeting thought that the Rexley fortune and titles would someday belong to Marie's children. Cyril was unlikely to give up his carefree life of gambling and mistresses for the stoic life of Society, and he, Jonathon, definitely had no head for attaching himself to one of the obnoxious, chatty virgins of the *ton*.

Bentley Smythe looked to Jonathon. "As you know, my lord, you have rights to the estate and all its holding as you will soon officially be named the new Lord Somerset." He inclined his head in the direction of Cyril. "Master Cyril, you shall be granted a generous allowance."

As Smythe relayed the sum of Cyril's portion, Lady Wescotte let out a gasp. Cyril cast her a crooked smile and when she turned to him, he cocked an eye at her. "Not to worry, Aunt Harriet. Papa was quite plump in the pocket. There is still some left for young Geoffry."

The boy had the decency to look embarrassed. Lady Wescotte did not. She was a puffed-up adder, Jonathon thought. She wanted something, the selfish dragon, and he was going to have to tolerate her until he could find out what it was.

"As for young Geoffry," Smythe went on, wisely ignoring the previous exchange, "there is a Sussex property which will be entrusted to me until such time as Geoffry reaches the age of two-and-twenty. Then it is his to do with as he chooses."

Geoffry seemed pleased enough with the allotted portion, but Lady Wescotte's chins reddened. Her body went stiff, as if it took all her energy to remain calm and ladylike. Jonathon ignored the harpy, knowing full well she was never satisfied with anything, and turned his attention back to the solicitor's instructions.

"Mrs. Marie Beauchamps is to receive all of the jewelry acquired by the late Lady Somerset except for those pieces that have been handed down through the generations. Those are to remain in the Rexley vault until such time as Jonathon, Lord Somerset, takes a wife."

With that announcement, Cyril laughed heartily. "Jonathon, take a wife? Poppycock! I would sooner take the King's shilling than my brother take a lady."

Jonathon glared at his outspoken brother but Cyril ignored the silent rebuke. "We shall be bachelors and cronies until our final breaths. I would be willing to lay certain odds on that."

Bentley Smythe ignored Cyril's outburst and spoke directly to Jonathon. "There are certain stipulations of which you and I must have a private audience, besides that, there are no further instructions."

Lady Wescotte twisted in her seat a little and smiled sweetly—a feat most difficult for the sour woman, and one that put the new lord immediately at daggers-drawn. "Jonathon...L-Lord Somerset...I pray you will also grant me a private audience with you?"

"Perhaps tomorrow," Jonathon replied. "The hour is late and we are all tired. If you have no objections, I would bid you wait until we have all had some rest."

"Indeed, my lord," the lady replied. She pulled herself out of the chair with her son's aid and started for the door.

"Aunt Harriet?" She turned around. "You have called me Jonathon all my life, why become so formal with me now?"

Lady Wescotte seemed to falter for a moment but regained her dignity without much delay. "You are a grown man with title and responsibility now, not some sapling in shortcoats."

"Ah. And you thought perhaps I needed to be reminded of that fact?" he asked pointedly.

"Not at all, my lord." She glanced around at everyone in the room. "But others might need the prompting. After all, with your inheritance comes the ability to make undisputed decisions."

He drew his brows together and studied her, puzzled

by her cryptic rebuttal. "Good night, Aunt Harriet," he said finally.

"Come along, Geoffry. I don't want to wander these haunted halls alone. Heaven knows if that awful ghost will abduct me," she muttered as she left the room with Geoffry in tow.

"Well, can't say as I understood any of that. She doesn't really believe in the Somerset Ghost does she? Why, everyone knows the old man invented that to scare off visitors," said Cyril, popping off the chair with agility. He muttered something about an old goat, and then turned to his cousin. "I shall be off to my bedchamber without further ado. Marie, would you like me to escort you to your room, or would you prefer the company of our auspicious Chauncy? Wouldn't want you pinched into the netherworld, now would we?"

Marie stood and took Cyril's proffered arm. "You are the wit's end, Cyril. That my brother had some of your sally."

"Ah, that my brother did, too, Cousin," Cyril remarked, opening the door to allow Marie exit, and casting an amused smile to Jonathon.

The new Lord Somerset ignored Cyril and turned his attention to the solicitor. As the door closed, Jonathon, spoke. "So what are these stipulations, Bentley? I don't have to cut off an arm or anything as ghastly, do I?"

Smythe hesitated, evidently not sharing in Jonathon's humour.

His smile faded as he sank onto the settee recently vacated by his brother. "All right, Smythe, what is it?"

"Well, my lord, it is thus. If you do not marry within the year, the barony will revert to Master Cyril." The words spewed forth at such a rate they seemed to run together. Jonathon, however, did not miss their interpretation.

Jonathon narrowed his gaze. "You are bamming, right? I mean, this has got to be a joke."

"Of course the title would remain yours. However, all holdings would transfer to your brother."

Jonathon leaned forward, laying an intense eye on the nervous countenance of the solicitor. "You are quite serious," he said.

"There is more, my lord. You must wed a certain Miss Lark Blackwell."

"What!" Lord Somerset sprang out of his seat, glared at Smythe. "This must be a ruse. You can't possibly mean to tell me that not only has my father made my marriage a condition of keeping the barony away from my wastrel of a brother, but he has personally named the wife I am supposed to take?" Lord Somerset's boots abused the rich burgundy rug as he paced the floor. "The man *was* insane. I never thought it, but he was." He spun to face the solicitor. "Who is this Lark...Lark..."

"Blackwell," Smythe replied with hesitation in his voice.

"Blackwell," Lord Somerset repeated on a breath of defeated air. He shook his dark head, his eyes probing that of the solicitor's. "Blackwell was the name of the house in which my mother was killed."

Smythe nodded. "Yes."

"There were no survivors of that house."

Smythe opened his mouth to speak, but Lord Somerset's biting oath silenced the man.

"This is the most ludicrous thing I have ever heard! Marry someone I know not?"

"It's not as if that sort of thing isn't done, my lord," Smythe ventured, fidgeting with his neckcloth.

"Damnation! What was the man thinking? He was *not* thinking, obviously. He knew I would never entrust the family reputation and wealth to Cyril. Always defended him, I did, and look what it has gotten me." He grunted. "And Lark Blackwell must be as insane as Papa had clearly become."

It was too much to fathom. He couldn't believe his father would arrange such a scheme on his own. Surely this Lark Blackwell had taken advantage of the old man's addled brain. Lord Somerset spun around and glared daggers at Smythe. "So who is she, Bentley? You might as well tell all."

Smythe's voice was no more than a whisper carried on the crackling of the fire. "The Somerset ghost, my Lord."

Chapter Two

Lark trembled in the darkened corner. She should have stepped forward long before now, but with so much activity, there had seemed to be no appropriate time. Besides, the menagerie of personalities that crowded the usually quiet library was such an invigorating change from her uneventful reality; she had lost herself in the play of events.

But now the new Lord Somerset looked as if he would strangle any chit who happened upon the misfortune of being named Lark, regardless of whether or not her family bore the name Blackwell. He already held her in contempt. Once he realized she'd been in the room the entire time, he would accuse her also of eavesdropping, even though she had been doing no such thing—*exactly*. Mr. Smythe had asked her to be present. She hadn't hidden in the corner deliberately—it had just turned out that way. The dim candlelight merely did not illuminate her seat. Uncertainty and fear bolted her bottom to the chair.

She needed to come forward now, but as she studied Jonathon Rexley's changing—ever hardening—expression as he opened the letter sealed with the Somerset crest that Smythe had handed him, her courage wavered, then dissolved.

Her heart pounded against her ribs. Oh, it was not supposed to be this way. She had dreamed of being his wife ever since she'd crept into his sickroom so long ago. Even wet with fever, his face had been compelling and kind—not like it was this minute. Although she could not remember much of her life before coming to live at Somerset Manor, he was one of the fond recollections.

Even at the age of five, she had loved him—a childish infatuation, to be true—but a tender pulling of the heartstrings, nonetheless. Ten years her senior, he had not even given her a glance. But later—when she had sneaked into his sickroom—he had gazed upon her as if she were an angel.

She had never forgotten that night, that look. It was what had made her agree to this addle-pated idea the late Lord Somerset had devised. She had convinced herself that Jonathon returned her affection. Obviously it was not so. The fire in his eye so many years ago had been the result of fever, not infatuation. He did not know she existed; Lord Peter had spun a terrible tale.

Regardless, she had to face the truth of things. No use putting it off. With a breath of resolve, she pulled herself out of the chair. At her movement, both men turned in her direction. She stepped forward into the light.

She smiled tentatively, expecting a full-scale attack from Lord Somerset. But he just stared at her.

Then his brow creased and his mouth opened, but before he could speak, Bentley Smythe maneuvered around him. "Ah, there you are, Miss Lark." He urged her forward with a wave of his hand. "Come, come. Do not be afraid. Lord Somerset here won't hurt you."

Lark wasn't so sure of that. As she stepped forward, her eyes never left the new lord of the manor. His gaze captivated her, all emotion hidden from his countenance. Still, from his outburst earlier, she knew he must be furious. Hesitantly, she came to stand before him then curtsied in respect.

Smythe was the one to break the silence that had consumed the room. "Jonathon, Lord Somerset, may I present Miss Lark Blackwell."

Ethereal. The word invaded Jonathon's mind the moment he laid eyes on Lark Blackwell. She seemed to float across the room, her white muslin gown flowing around her, caressing her legs as a cool breeze touches the cheek on a hot summer's day. Her hair, adorned with a ring of fresh flowers, shone the colour of the sun at its hottest white, her skin the palest alabaster.

No wonder she had been redubbed the Somerset Ghost. She was otherworldly. But *angel* would have been a more appropriate moniker. She was beautiful, not frightening. Drinking in the sight of her awakened

15

feelings he didn't know he had—chivalrous, protective desires...and something more base, more passionate. The yen to reach out, lift her into his arms, and carry her off to private a rendezvous began to melt his anger, and he immediately knew he needed to be wary of this bewitching creature.

He stiffened his spine and schooled his countenance. "You have been hiding in the shadows like a rat, Miss Blackwell. What say you of this? Did you know of my father's plans to saddle us together? Did you have act in them?"

As he fired questions at her, she shook her head adamantly, her face strained with evident worry. He ignored it, refusing to be swayed by feminine wiles.

"Why do you not speak, vixen? Do you not realize you will never prevail? Answer my queries." He quieted for a moment and studied her teary-eyed mien.

She looked like a chastised child, and for a moment, he felt a twinge of guilt at crucifying her. He opened his mouth to speak, but Smythe touched his arm, drew his attention. He scarcely had time to comprehend what was happening before Lark picked up her skirt and fled the room.

Stunned, Jonathon stared at the solicitor. He raised an inquiring eyebrow, and Smythe referred to the sealed letter. "Read the missive, my lord. I trust it will explain everything better than I."

Jonathon settled into the gilt-edged chair and stared at his father's handwriting. The letters were strong and steady—not as one would expect from an ailing man. The ink began to blur as Jonathon scrutinized the page without focus of eye or mind. What could his father have meant in saddling him with a bride he had never met?

He scanned the paper, first for key words such as "marriage" and "Blackwell", then more closely. As nothing made sense, Jonathon's icy rage began to melt away.

My dearest Jonathon,

I have been quite secretive since the passing of your mother and you have been the utmost best son. I do realize how difficult it has been for you to have an insane father. However, as I explain, I hope you will see it was all for the best.

16

As you already know, Drew Blackwell and I were the closest of friends. He saved my life in that dratted war with the traitorous Americas. What I did, and what I ask you to do, is for his memory and that of your beloved mother.

It is with a leadened heart I reveal to you the fire that consumed your mother was not merely the accident of a careless servant. It was a deliberate act, a heinous plot.

I quite understand that it will be at best difficult for you to understand why I ask of you what I am about to ask. Realize these are not the ramblings of an old insane fool on his deathbed, but rather that of a strong-minded man who divulges this to you with free-will, knowing one day my life will end and you must carry out my wishes...

He raised his eyes to Smythe. "Just how long ago did Papa pen this?"

The solicitor glanced down at the paper, then back at Jonathon. "I assure you, my lord, it was before he became quite ill."

"You know what this says, then?"

Smythe's balding head lowered in a slight nod. "I have not read the missive word for word, my lord, but Lord Somerset did explain the situation to me—in the strictest of confidences, assuredly," he quickly added.

"Of course, of course," Jonathon muttered, moving his attention back to his father's written explanation...

I have kept the secret close to my heart and now I must ask you to do the same. There was a small girl in the house that night. You remember her; she was as a sister to you in days past—An eager child wanting to stay out of her bedchamber because her favorite "aunt" was visiting. Lark's disobedience kept harm at bay. I have kept her safe since, and now I must ask the same of you. Marry her, Jonathon, and she will become Lady Somerset. No one need know of her past. A marriage to keep her safe, Jonathon. Not a true marriage, just one to keep her safe. In memory of me. In memory of your mother. I implore you. Marry her and let no one know of her true identity.

****

Outside the library, Lark searched the great room for her abigail, frantic for some comfort from the woman who had been with her since birth. Fury and fear bubbled their way to her throat as she ran above stairs into her suite of rooms in the unused wing of Somerset Manor. There, her maid attended to straightening the clothes in the wardrobe.

Rebekka turned to face her mistress. "There you are, dear miss," the plump woman said. "You look a fright. 'Tis an awful thing to have to endure, what?"

Lark frowned, ignoring the woman's comment. "You must come with me now, Rebekka," she said with hand gestures. "You must make him understand. Oh, Lord Peter said all would work out for the best, but he was wrong. He thinks I am the devil's spawn. I see it in his eyes. The accusation. The contempt."

Rebekka took Lark's hands in her own, silencing the younger woman's words. "There, there, miss. I don't know what you're on about, but I can see you are quite overset. Lead me where you will, and together we will see. Have we not been seeing to things together since you were a little one?"

Rebekka trailed behind as Lark raced down the spiral staircase.

She stopped with her hand on the knob of the closed library doors, her breath coming in short ineffective bursts. Rebekka laid a hand on Lark's muslin sleeve.

"I do not think you have anything to worry about, m'lady. Lord Peter would never marry you to an ogre." The abigail stepped back and motioned with an incline of the head for Lark to open the door.

She glanced from Rebekka's hand to the ornate doorknob. She had always trusted Lord Peter and could not think of a valid reason why she should not in this, but what if he'd been mistaken? Perhaps...

Without warning, the knob was ripped out of her hand, and the door flew open.

"Chauncy," Jonathon bellowed.

Lark's eyes moved from the unstarched silk cravat up to the hard face of Jonathon Rexley. Instinctively, she stepped back.

Off balance, she bumped into Rebekka. The older woman let out a tiny squeal.

Quick as lightening, Lord Somerset caught Lark's arm, kept her from falling. For an instant, time seemed to stand still as momentum sent Lark crashing into his chest. She inhaled the scent of him, consciously imbibed the heat of his gentle, steadying touch. She closed her eyes.

Then she was free and almost staggering once again from the abruptness of his release.

"Miss Blackwell. What is the meaning of your constant eavesdropping? If you are to be my wife you must gather some manners."

His words hadn't the time to sink into her mind before Lady Wescotte's shrill gasp echoed through the great room.

"Wife? You are taking a wife, Jonathon—L-lord Somerset?" Lady Wescotte's surprise registered on her elevated eyebrows.

"Must I reprimand two females today for listening when their ears should have been tightly closed?" Lord Somerset tilted his face to the landing of the stairs where Lady Wescotte stood, one hand on the carved banister, the other planted firmly on her bulging hip.

A disgusted groan escaped Lady Wescotte's mouth. "I merely came to see what all the disturbance was about. Heavens, it sounded as if there were an army of soldiers bounding above and below stairs."

"'Twas nothing, save the Somerset Ghost," Jonathon replied.

"Nonsense," Lady Wescotte remarked, obviously offended by his patronizing comment.

He looked pointedly at Lark. "Am I not correct?"

Her cheeks burned. Never before had she wanted so much to strike at someone. Jonathon Rexley was heartless. She knew the rumors. He knew the rumors. How she had looked forward to hiding no longer, only to be ridiculed and dared by his laughing obsidian eyes. Rage forced its way from her stomach to her throat, but then his eyes softened. He slightly inclined his head and Lark found her anger softening with his countenance.

He turned back to Lady Wescotte. "All right Aunt Harriet, if you must know what all the commotion is about, I shall tell you." He took up Lark's hand in his own. She stared at where they were joined, amazed at how dwarfed his strong hand made hers appear. She swallowed a lump of emotion and looked up into his face. "Miss Lark Black—"

At that moment, Smythe emerged in the doorway of the library. "Blackburn," he said over Jonathon's tongue. "Miss Lark Blackburn." The lawyer bowed to the lovely miss. "It is nice to see you once again."

Lark endowed the bald man with a crooked smile. She had made his acquaintance not ten minutes past, what was his game, and why had he referred to her with a fictitious surname?

Jonathon inclined his head slightly, in deference to the solicitor's fortuitous interruption. He was a fool. After reading his father's letter, He should have known better than to use the chit's real name, even though only family was present. He directed his gaze back to his awaiting aunt, training his voice to be steady and true, and showing no hint that Blackburn was not what he had intended to utter all along. "Miss Blackburn here, was so taken by my proffer of marriage, that she bounded up the staircase like an excited child to tell her—closest friend," he frowned passively as he glanced at Rebekka, "and abigail," he gazed back up the stairs, "that the honorable Lord Somerset had extended the invitation."

He smiled down at Lark. "Is that not the case, my sweet?" He hoped to heaven and beyond, Harriet did not ask why the abigail was above stairs—or why Lark was in attendance, for that matter.

Lark's eyes were as vast as the blue oceans. Slowly, her head bobbed an affirmative answer and he gave her hand, now ensconced in both of his, a little squeeze.

"There you have it, Aunt Harriet."

The plump woman hastened down the stairs. Her oversized skirts rustled and the jewelry about her body jingled with the quickness of her step. "But you have never mentioned this woman before. Who is she? From whence did she come? When did you court her? What did you say her name was? Well, never mind."

As she reached the bottom of the staircase, Lady Wescotte stopped, an almost satisfied expression settling over her face. Then she smiled and clapped her hands together.

"Miss, I am so relieved that a woman as lovely as you

has finally brought my Jonathon to his senses."

"'My Jonathon' is it?" All eyes turned to Cyril, who was now draped across the banister. "I am quite taken aback by all the events of the day." He put a dramatic hand to his forehead then acted as if he might swoon. "By Jove, Jon has gone from beloved nephew to respected lord and back. And, I must say, if I had wagered against his ever finding a wife, I would be registering to take the King's shilling this very moment."

"Ninnyhammer," Lady Wescotte rebuked. "Stop acting the fool and welcome Miss Blackburn into the family."

"You have certainly turned congenial of a sudden, Aunt Harriet. I would think this turn of events weakens your position, not strengthens it." Cyril started down the stairs.

"Cyril, you go too far."

He met Jonathon's censure with a resigned smile. "No doubt, brother mine. But give me credit for being quite consistent." He turned to Lark and bowed politely. "Cyril Rexley, at your service." He raised his eyes to hers. "Forgive my ill manners. I am not used to being in the company of such a lovely, refined woman. Jonathon is but a lucky man."

Colour reddened Lark's cheeks and Jonathon thought that perhaps marrying such a lovely creature would not be such drudgery after all.

Chapter Three

"You bellowed, my lord?" Chauncy's bland countenance belied the sarcasm of his words.

"Yes, Chauncy, that I did. Bring us crystal flutes and the best champagne in the cellar. We have a betrothal to celebrate." Jonathon's gaze lowered and settled upon Lark's face. She wondered what thoughts roamed the rooms of his mind. His eyes glowed of pleasantries. She smiled at him—a smile she hoped conveyed her desire to please him. He blinked rapidly then tore his gaze from her. Dropping her hand, he turned and started back into the library.

Lady Wescotte was quick off her mark, coming within an ames ace of crushing Lark's toes. Lark stepped back and let the Lady waddle after Jonathon. To be sure, Lark was still fuzzy from the stolen warmth of his hand. He had bestowed on her such a caring gaze, and then dropped her hand as if it were riddled with disease. Bemused by his performance, she wondered if this was how all lords behaved. Certainly, Lord Peter had never treated her with such contradiction.

The touch of Rebekka's hand to Lark's elbow brought the young miss out of her musings.

The abigail nodded. "Go in, Miss. This is what it's all about. Do not be afeared, I am right behind you."

With that assurance, Lark was comforted only a little. No other person had been with her all her life. Only Rebekka understood Lark's hand-language—and only in that woman did Lark have complete and utter trust. In fact, had it not been for the abigail's quick-wittedness and lack of regard for her own safety, Lark might have suffered the same fate as that of the rest of her family. She felt a bond to the woman that exceeded mere gratitude. Still, she wasn't sure anyone could shield her from the seesaw emotions induced in her by Jonathon Rexley. One moment hope filled her, the next vexation.

She took a steadying breath and, with Rebekka close behind, entered the library that would never greet her with the same contentment it had before the developments of this eve.

Lord Somerset—Jonathon—the name strolled through Lark's mind with ease. She liked his name, Jonathon Rexley, and wished she had the ability to utter it. Perhaps then, this entire situation would be easier.

Lord Somerset had situated himself in the very spot she had first witnessed him—in front of the fireplace. Mr. Cyril Rexley had taken the seat formerly occupied by Lady Wescotte, and the woman stood over him, trilling something about not liking the settee by the hearth.

Cyril murmured unintelligibly and lifted himself out of the chair to cross the room. "Miss Blackburn, do come sit by the fireplace on the settee. I daresay it's the most comfortable in the place." He shot a saucy look to Lady Wescotte that Jonathon evidently noticed.

"Do try to behave, Cyril, if not for my sake then for that of my lovely betrothed," Jonathon rebuffed.

"My apologies indeed, Miss Blackburn. I assure you once again, I am unaccustomed to such refinery in a woman."

Lark's cheeks grew warm, and she avoided Cyril's gaze. She heard the breath expel from Lord Somerset, and from under lowered lashes, witnessed the exasperated look with which he seared his brother. She had no idea how to take it all.

She raised her head and showed Rebekka a pleading countenance. The abigail turned up the corners of her mouth, and signed, "As I have said, not to worry. Sit and be welcomed."

"What is that you do?" Harriet, Lady Wescotte inquired of the lady's maid.

Rebekka slightly dipped one knee. "Nothing ill m'lady, I assure you. I was just speaking with my charge. She lives a quiet life."

Lady Wescotte turned questioning eyes to her eldest nephew. "She speaks in riddles," she trilled, her voice squeaky with exasperation. "What does the woman mean?"

A sliver of anxiety wound its way round Jonathon's

heart as he glanced at Rebekka then turned his attention to his fiancée. She was perched on the settee in the most ladylike of poses, a paragon of beauty. Innocence exuded from her with the ease of rain from a plump cloud. Her sky blue eyes bespoke every thought that rambled through her pretty head. Apprehension dulled their brightness, and after gaining the knowledge that she had been locked in this old house since she was a tot, he could fully understand her uncertainty.

He supposed it was his responsibility to come up with a plausible response to Aunt Harriet's inquiry, but he could not very well come out and say, *not to worry, Auntie, Papa had this young sprite locked away with him these years past and thus the gel has led a quiet life,* now could he? Besides, something dreadful and unspoken told him that wasn't to what the abigail referred.

He groaned inwardly, opened his mouth then clamped it shut. He had not an appropriate thought in his head. He opened his mouth a second time, but Rebekka took a step forward and spoke. "It is quite unfortunate I must inform you that Miss Lark is unable to speak."

"What?" The word sprung forth from Jonathon's lips like a jack out of the box. It gave fright even to himself.

Cyril laughed. "Surprise to all, I see."

Jonathon found he couldn't move. His ribs felt as if they might collapse at any moment. In truth, he wasn't sure they hadn't already collapsed. He shifted his gaze to Smythe who had the decency to look sheepish, and then he glared at Lark. Innocent! He had actually thought her innocent? She was part of a scheme, no doubt. A wily, deficient gel that had convinced his papa to marry her off. By Jove! He'd been henpecked even without his knowledge. He would have to find a way out of this mess. He couldn't wed a deficient gel, no matter how pretty she might be. He had worked too hard to earn respectability after his papa had gone off his rocker. He could not risk all he had worked for—not even to save the family fortune from his irresponsible brother.

Lady Wescotte wiggled her way out of the chair, her massive jowls rippling like the waters of the Thames on a windy day.

"Surely you cannot mean to wed the deficient girl?"

she wailed.

"Aunt!" Cyril cut in. "I do believe the lady said the miss was unable to speak. She did not mention an impairment of her hearing."

Lady Wescotte looked on Lark with toplofty cordiality. "Sorry, my dear, but of course you understand my concern for my nephew. Should he buckle himself to one so all abroad, it would surely be frowned upon. "Why," she returned her gaze to Jonathon, "what *would* people say?"

Aunt Harriet spoke the truth of it, but he couldn't very well allow her to insult his future wife in front of others. After all, what would people say to that? It offended his every feeling to think of wedding someone the likes of Lark, but he had to keep up appearances until he could find a way out of the predicament. He looked pointedly at his dragon of an aunt. "Must I remind you, you are addressing my betrothed? I daresay you should show a bit more respect."

Lark listened to the exchange in utter distress. Lord Peter had been so very wrong when he said Jonathon held her in high regard. Not only did Jonathon not love her, he did not even like her. The lines straining his features betrayed that truth, even while he so gallantly defended her to Lady Wescotte.

Jonathon continued to reprimand his aunt's behavior, and Cyril touched a gentle fingertip to Lark's forearm and spoke in hushed tones. "Chin up, my girl, Aunt Harriet cannot say a kind word to a soul. Jon loves you, he must do, so don't worry about the old cantankerous cabbage head. We've all had a go round with her at one time or another."

Lark looked to Rebekka for reassurance and although the companion lent her a smile, Lark could see it was not one so full of confidence.

"Now, if you would be so kind Aunt Harriet, I would appreciate it if you would act as hostess in this matter and fetch my cousins so that they, too, might share in this news which just might prove to lighten the dismal occasion of my father's death." Lord Somerset dismissed his aunt directly then proffered his hand to Lark. "Come, my dear, stand at my side so that everyone might see just how unified we are."

"Here, here," Cyril intoned, raising his empty hand in a toast of sorts.

Lady Wescotte witnessed the exchange with obvious vexation. Her stance spoke the most unladylike urge to belt her nephew a good one.

Then, as quickly as she had riled, her reddened countenance faded and, as if claiming an impending victory, she waddled out of the room.

Jonathon leaned down and whispered in Lark's ear. "Do not mistake the reprimand of my aunt's behavior as acceptance of you, you little minx. We shall get to the bottom of your and my father's scheming just as soon as I have dealt with my family. I have worked too long and hard to wind up saddled with a conniving wench the likes of you."

Time stood still. How could he be so harsh? She had not schemed, had not planned. It had all been Lord Peter's idea. She fought the tears that threatened with every ounce of strength she could summon. All she had ever wanted was to be normal.

Chauncy arrived with a cart of champagne and crystal as voices filtered in from the great room. Marie barreled through first. "What is this Mama tells me of a marriage, Jonathon?"

Lord Somerset drew his attention from Lark and tossed a scathing look at Lady Wescotte as she jaunted in behind her daughter.

"I trust it was not a secret, my lord," Lady Wescotte crooned. She glanced over her shoulder. "Come, come, Geoffry, do not linger."

Geoffry remained in the shadows by the door while Lady Wescotte settled into her favorite chair. Marie made her way to Jonathon and smiled brightly. "So this is your betrothed, I take it." She turned loving blue eyes on Lark and curtsied in greeting. "It certainly is a pleasure to meet the young lady who stole my Jonathon's heart."

Lark showed her to-be cousin a broad smile, but inside she did not feel at all like smiling. For once, she felt as if a case of the vapors would be a welcome respite from all the people in the room. Was this how her life was to proceed? One person after another approaching, welcoming, criticizing? She would wind up going mad. If she could not compose her nerves around the likes of her family, how was she to handle Society?

She attempted to calm herself with a steadying breath. Marie seemed quite polite and smiled in a way that was not at all intimidating. Cyril had acted the perfect gentleman, even going so far as to criticize his own aunt in order to bring Lark to ease, yet she still found the urge to shed tears nearly all-consuming.

Again, she doubted Lord Peter's judgment, but quickly chided herself. After all, he had preserved her life and her future. Surely, he had known what would be best.

Her dilemma overwhelmed her. She glanced up at Lord Somerset and studied his profile as he answered Marie's query about the impending marriage. He had quite a way about him, so commanding, so steely. What had happened to the Jonathon she had fallen in love with as a child, the Jonathon who had looked at her with awe from his sick bed? He had been replaced by this hardened stone.

It was going to be impossible to marry him when she knew he would forever be ashamed of her.

Jonathon looked down at his bride and felt a smile pull at the corners of his lips as she quickly averted her gaze. He found it quite disturbing that simply catching her studying him issued a distinct swell of pleasure within, but he could not deny the sensation. She was the same angel who had looked at him with concern when he lay feverish and delirious. Yet, now he knew her as an obvious wangling chit, he could not allow himself to be swayed by her innocent looks and angelic smile. He sucked in a deep breath and readied himself for battle.

He looked to Aunt Harriet and cleared his throat. "As you all know," he eyed Lady Wescotte pointedly, "I have decided to take a wife. May I present my betrothed, Miss Lark Blackburn." As a murmur of congratulations circulated the library, he uncorked the champagne.

Jonathon distributed the filled glasses one by one, and Cyril proposed a toast that included continued life and happiness to the couple. All seemed content until Lady Wescotte parted her lips.

"By the Bye, Jonathon, when do you expect this

betrothal to take place? This family is in mourning, if I may be so bold as to remind you."

"Allow me to assure you, Aunt, that as it is my own father who is gone aloft, it is quite unnecessary for you to remind me I am in mourning. I daresay my heart does that for me." He scanned the room, dismissing any more Lady Wescotte might have to say on the matter. "Now that we are all acquainted, I suggest we retire for the evening. I would remind you all of the prudence in keeping my betrothal ensconced within these walls until such time as is appropriate to pursue a public announcement." Without waiting for the assent to his request, he turned his attention to the solicitor. "If you could remain for a few moments longer, I would like to have a word."

The remainder of the family gave their regards and left Jonathon alone with his betrothed and Bentley Smythe.

"Rebekka?" Jonathon set his gaze on the abigail. "I would that you wait in the great room for Miss Blackburn."

Rebekka bobbed a curtsey and complied.

Jonathon took Lark's hand and guided her once again to the nearby settee. "Please do sit, Miss Blackburn. I'm sure today has been quite an ordeal for you."

Lark settled onto the settee with a wariness in her soul unmatched by anything she had before experienced. How could he act so outwardly pleasant, then whisper hate and contempt into her ear? She should have ignored her childish fantasies and refused this farce of a marriage. It was just that she couldn't remember much of her life before her parent's death, and she longed so much to recapture some small part of that—with someone who *could* remember. Someone like the romanticized Jonathon who would love her, and teach her, and make her life normal.

"All right, Smythe, what the devil is going on?" Lord Somerset's booming voice reverberated from the cavern of the fireplace and snapped Lark's wandering into focus. "Did you know of this, this *woman's* deficiency?"

Smythe looked so forlorn that Lark felt sorry for the man. He glanced at her with nervous eyes then turned back to the forbidding Lord Somerset. "Yes, my lord. Of course I knew," he replied on a nod.

"Why then did you not disclose this most important information?" Jonathon shot back at the balding man.

"There was not time, my lord."

Jonathon flung a pointed finger in Lark's direction. Instinctively she cringed back as if he would actually strike her. "Do you expect me to believe it was an oversight that you kept her a secret?" He raked a hand through his impeccably styled hair and spun around to show them both his back. "What in tarnation was my father thinking? He knew what his eccentricity did to us. He knew what it took me to regain respect. Why would he do this?" He turned to face the solicitor once again. "You find a way around this, Smythe. And you do it post haste."

Lark could not take any more. She stood and made short order of crossing the room.

"Where do you think you are going?" Lord Somerset bellowed from behind her.

She ignored him and opened the door, motioning for Rebekka. The abigail entered while Lark's hands flew in speech.

"But you must," Rebekka told her. Lark adamantly shook her head.

"I will not!" she told her abigail. "Now translate what I said, or I shall find another way."

Rebekka sighed and turned to the gentlemen. "My lady wishes to inform you. . ."

Lark touched Rebekka's arm then signed, "You translate *exactly* what I said," she warned, knowing full well that Rebekka tended to sweet-coat her translations.

"Yes, yes, all right." The abigail looked at Lord Somerset. "Miss Lark says she would not marry you were you the last man on God's green earth."

Chapter Four

Lord Somerset suffered a fitful night. He laid awake most of it, his mind alert with the problems facing him in the next six months and beyond. He still could not fully comprehend his father's intentions, nor the source of the apparent danger to Lark's life should her identity be revealed. His father had put him in a quandary, and now he had to figure his own way out of the blasted mess. He could not marry Lark, but he could not jeopardize the family estate either. And, neither could he allow Lark's life to remain in danger—no matter how ill he felt about her. It was just not in him to discard her without care.

As the new day dawned, he almost looked forward to the triviality of playing host to his family. Lark was safely locked in the unused portion of the manor, and as Smythe had pointed out last evening, if she had been able to keep herself hidden these many years, the fortnight his family remained in residence should be kindly done.

Jonathon considered it a welcome reprieve not to have to deal with the little chit for a while. Although, he still had Aunt Harriet to attend, he had not forgotten.

Impeccably dressed in a rich forest green velvet coat and gray britches, he felt more comfortably in control as he made his way below stairs and into the dining room. The rest of the family had obviously been awaiting his arrival, and as his gaze fell on Aunt Harriet, he felt as if he had just been entrapped in the snare of a fowler.

Cyril, seated to the right of the table head, threw his brother a rather contemptible glare, and since Jonathon had neither seen nor spoken to his brother since last evening, he had no inkling as to what he had done to deserve such a look.

Aunt Harriet, seated in a most unfortunate position next to Cyril, opened her mouth and raised a finger. He was not in the mood for the woman's prattle.

"I trust our meeting can be postponed until after the morning meal, Aunt Harriet?" He asked, allowing the derision in his tone to squelch her penchant for taking control.

"Of course, Lord Som…Jonathon. It would not have crossed my mind to interrupt the morning gathering. We are together as a whole family so little these days." She gave him the most sweet-coated of smiles.

His stomach lurched, and he swallowed the biting need to issue a snide remark.

"So kind of you to think of the family first, Aunt Harriet," Cyril put in.

"You question my sincerity?" Lady Wescotte inquired, sounding quite rebuffed.

"I can honestly tell you, Aunt, I never once questioned your sincerity."

Jonathon stifled the grin that teased the corners of his mouth and took his place at the head of the table. "Good morning Marie, Geoffry."

"Good morning, Jon," Marie answered cheerfully.

"I trust you all slept well? I cannot tell you what a comfort it has been in this time of mourning to have you all near me."

"Is that because it has been no comfort at all?"

Marie sniggered. "You are completely incorrigible, Cyril Rexley. Completely too much."

Cyril bowed his head. "Thank you," he said with mock reverence. "I do try very hard to live up to my reputation."

"Perhaps you should try living up to the reputation of someone else," Lady Wescotte spat. She sucked in a breath that seemed as if it would empty the room of oxygen then let it out at gale force. "Do pass that dish of butter, Geoffry. I believe if I do not get some nourishment soon, I will wither away."

Cyril laughed outright. "My dear Aunt, you could make it to the turn of the century without food and still not wither away."

"Cyril!" Jonathon might agree with his brother's assessment of Aunt Harriet's lack of sincerity, as well as her abundance of flesh, but he couldn't condone the blatant disrespect upon which his younger brother insisted.

Cyril afforded his aunt a contrite look. "I apologize for my outburst. It was merely a jest. You know I would never poke fun at you in any company outside the family."

Lady Wescotte glanced at the family members present, her eyes resting on Jonathon. For an odd moment, he felt a compassion for her he had never before experienced. She looked truly undone. Her eyes seemed to glaze into a retreated battle status—but then, without much delay, she steeled them once more and moved her gaze to Cyril. "It is a pity your mother didn't live long enough to teach you how to treat a lady."

The harshness of her words did not escape Jonathon, nor did they surprise him. His aunt had always been adept at issuing cutting remarks without remorse. He should rebuff her, he knew, but rather than prolong a conversation whose end was long overdue, he called the morning meal to order and tried to avoid dialogue of any sort. He would deal with Harriet, *Lady Wescotte*, later.

****

The aged afternoon found Jonathon alone in his study. Regardless of how many times he reviewed his father's missive, or the terms of the will, he could not find any loopholes or answers. He would have to marry Lark Blackwell in order to keep the Rexley fortune and reputation from his irresponsible brother.

It was difficult to believe it had been Lark who sneaked into his bedroom that night when he was ill, she who touched him so gently and looked deep into his fevered face with such compassion and longing. How he had wanted her then.

Oh, how the reality of her, scheming and deficient, fell short of his fevered expectations. If only she had turned out to be the angelic being he'd concocted—the cherubic creature she appeared to be outwardly—then perhaps he could resolve to follow his father's wishes.

A determined rap on the mahogany door dissolved his musings. "Yes," he answered hesitantly. It didn't take a sixth sense for him to know it was Lady Wescotte. She had attempted to nab him now and then all morning, and he had successfully avoided her until now.

The door opened, and she waddled her pudgy frame

through the opening. She reminded him of an oversized mallard, but he refused even to dwell on the thought. In truth, he felt sorry for the woman. She was accepted by Society solely because she was Wescotte's wife, and tolerated by family only because common blood ran through their veins. It was a rather unappealing existence—one Jonathon would wish on no one.

The fact that marrying a deficient girl such as Lark would put him in a similar position was quite ironic and did not escape his notice.

"Ah, there you are my dear nephew. I am so pleased we finally have the opportunity to speak without prying ears to overhear our private conversation."

"Is this to be a private conversation, then, Aunt Harriet?"

She made her way to the leather wing chair opposite him, and, putting a stack of neatly disguised papers on his desk in front of her, sat down. The leather let out a groan of protest under her weight as she shifted to a comfortable position and smoothed out the ample material in her skirts.

Jonathon waited patiently for his aunt to settle herself. When she had, she looked on him with as much a sorrowful gaze as she could impart.

Her insincerity sickened his stomach.

"You are Lord Somerset now, my dear Jonathon, and as much as it pains me to do so, I do believe you need to know the truth of all matters concerning your family and estate." She paused for breath and effect and a knot bowed in Jonathon's throat.

"What is it you think I should know, Aunt Harriet?" he managed to ask while silently praying it had nothing to do with her possibly having discovered that Lark actually resided in his home. For Harriet to hold such damaging news was a danger. Not that he thought she would start a family scandal—unless, perchance it would benefit herself.

"Well, I am not sure where to begin, Jonathon, it is a rather, shall we say, *delicate*, situation." She probed him with her eyes, for some reaction, he was sure, but he refused to give her the satisfaction; thus far, she had said absolutely nothing.

"I am quite positive it would be appropriate to begin at the beginning," he said evenly. "You do not mind if I take a drink while we converse, I trust?" He rose before she had the time to reply and made his way to the corner bar. "Would you care for something, Aunt? I could ring Chauncy to bring in some tea." He glanced at her over his shoulder.

"Nothing at all." He heard the groaning of the chair as she shifted her weight. "Well, the beginning. Let me see."

She still had her ringed finger to her lips in apparent deep thought when Jonathon returned to his seat. He wondered what could be so "delicate" that even Aunt Harriet could not bring herself to utter the words. He couldn't remember a time when the dragon had been rendered speechless, and he grew more and more apprehensive as the silence stretched on.

It was annoying, he finally concluded. Not frightening. Not intimidating. Merely, annoying. She sat there like a butcher waiting to chop off the chicken's head. Well, he would sooner be nabbed by robbers than stick his own neck under the hatchet. He sipped on his sherry with mustered calm.

"I suppose I must start at the beginning." She sighed as if this fact, a fact Jonathon had voiced what seemed like eons ago, pained her greatly and took much effort on her part.

He sat with his back as straight as a train rail and his expression just as unbending. He sipped again on the warm sherry.

"You see, Jonathon, it is Geoffry. Harold is not his father," she blurted out.

Jonathon's composure went awry. Sherry threatened to spill forth from his lips as he tried desperately not to choke. He managed to swallow the liquid without too much trouble. "What are you trying to say, Aunt Harriet? That he...that you..."

Lady Wescotte's eyes bulged with understanding. "No, no," she assured him hastily. "You misconstrue me. Neither am I his mother," she elaborated. "No one besides your father and me— and now you, of course—knows this. Neither Geoffry nor Marie has the slightest inclination.

34

We all thought the less that had knowledge, the better."

Jonathon studied his aunt. For a moment that she seemed truly uncomfortable, yet he knew right through to his bones that she had an ulterior motive for this conversation. She wanted something from him, but he could not comprehend just what *he* could possibly have to do with Geoffry being an adopted child.

He emptied the contents of his glass into his mouth. "Why are you telling me this?"

Lady Wescotte expelled a large amount of breath. "Geoffry's father was your own."

Chapter Five

Her declaration rose and hung in the silence between them. Time crawled on its belly, frightfully slow, and with caution.

Jonathon did not know whether to believe her or have her flogged. The latter truly would be deserved. He was never one silly enough to believe his father did not have faults, but loyalty was definitely not one of them—especially after he had evidently sacrificed much for the sole good of Lark, a child whom was not his own.

But why would Aunt Harriet lie—a bald-faced lie such as this, and against her own brother? Even the likes of she would not do such a thing. There would be no advantage in it.

It was Lady Wescotte who risked piercing the heavy silence. "I know it must be difficult for you, but, on my life, it is the truth."

Jonathon's thoughts clanged to a close. He felt the heat rise within him, creeping up his neck, consuming his ears. "It *will* be your life, Aunt Harriet, if this is not the truth." He held his voice even and deadly, his eyes steely and implacable. She needed to know it was a fool's errand she was carrying, if this not be the truth.

Her eyes darted nervously for a moment before she inched her way forward in the chair. "I thought you might not believe me, so I carried along the proof," she said, her tone now back to business.

Jonathon looked on while his aunt shuffled through the documents she had placed on his desk. It occurred to him then that she had been clutching these same papers while Smythe had read the terms of Peter Rexley's Will.

The rustle of the papers grated on his over-sensitized nerves, and the urge to rip the information from her chubby hands germinated inside him. He worked the muscle in his jaw to keep from carrying out the heinous deeds his mind concocted.

"Ah, here are the ones I seek," she said with satisfaction. She handed him the sheaf of papers and settled back into the chair.

The whine of the leather irritated his every sense, his usually unruffled composure gone to vacation.

"They should show you all you need to know."

He read the first document with much interest. It was a birth certificate naming some unbeknownst woman as the mother of "Geoffry Hammond". "Father" was listed as unknown. He raised his gaze to Lady Wescotte but she stopped him from speaking.

"Before you say a word, look at the other document."

He slid the birth certificate to the back and gazed at what appeared to be an adoption decree. It named Harold and Harriet Wescotte as the legal parents of one Geoffry Hammond, newly named Geoffry Wescotte. An addendum was attached that instructed one Peter Rexley, Lord Somerset, to pay an annual sum of one hundred guineas until Geoffry reached the age of ten and seven.

Disbelief dueled with acceptance inside him.

"So you see, Jonathon, I was quite on the up and up."

His gaze darted to Lady Wescotte. She looked quite satisfied with herself, which tweaked Jonathon's already shortened temper.

"What do you want, Aunt Harriet?" He bit out.

She started, and he felt a twinge of satisfaction at having shaken her with his caustic tone. She had no regard whatsoever, and he did not feel like extending her any courtesy. His father was gone aloft; it accomplished naught good to reveal the man's sins, save cause anguish to his family, so why would she do this now? It was heartless and cruel.

"W-well, to see to it you fulfill the terms of your father's agreement. It is the proper thing to do, you know." She seemed quite surprised to have to utter her request aloud.

The blood pounded in his ears. As if he needed to be reminded of his responsibilities! He had done nothing but fulfill responsibilities since the day his father saw fit to lock himself behind the walls of Somerset Manor. And now, on top of it all, Harriet the Fatted Hen had just laid this egg. Fulfilling responsibility was the last thing Jonathon wanted to do, but regardless of the turmoil churning within him, he knew responsibility was what he was going to deal with. Like it or not, that was the stuff he was made of.

He pushed the chair away from the desk and stood. Glancing at his empty sherry glass, the fleeting desire to be more like one of Cyril's cronies waltzed through the halls of his mind. How nice it would be to drown his responsibility in a bottle of sherry—or brandy—or a good stout port, for that matter.

He dropped the papers. "Leave these here with me and I will see to them and get back to you."

She struggled to her feet. "But, but..."

He let out an impatient sigh. "But what, Aunt Harriet?"

"These are my only copies," she said with deflated vehemence.

Unblemished rage consumed Jonathon's body, the pulse in his head boxing his temples. "Are you insinuating I might destroy them?"

"Of course not, Jonathon. No need to get testy. I am quite sure you are an honorable man." Silence hung like the blade of a guillotine. "Well, I shall leave you to it then," she ventured, although she remained motionless.

At length, she inched her way around the chair. "Yes, I shall leave you to it."

****

The sun hung low in the western sky and the air caught a chill. Still, Jonathon sat in the quiet solitude of his study. There were moments when he could hear Marie or Cyril, or some other member of the household making their way past his door, but no one dared enter, and he had no inclination of leaving his solace.

A determined rapping came at the door but Jonathon ignored it. Moments later, it came again.

"What is it?" He bellowed impatiently.

Chauncy opened the door and came in with a polite bow. "The others are preparing to take tea. Would you care for any my lord?"

"No." Jonathon did not favor his butler with a glance.

"Would you care for me to build a fire? There is quite

a chill in the air this eve."

"I am well aware of the weather, Chauncy. Leave me be."

"Very well, my lord."

Jonathon listened for the doors to click closed before he ventured to look about the room. The shadows had grown long, and despite his thick velvet coat, he could distinguish the drop in temperature. He had no inkling as to how long he had been sitting, staring, sifting through the papers his aunt had left him.

If he were to believe what he had read, Bentley Smythe knew all about this sordid little deed in which the late Lord Somerset had been involved. Jonathon wondered to how many other little family secrets Bentley Smythe was privy. The solicitor must not have exaggerated at all when he had said he was more than family solicitor to the Rexley household. By Jove, he had enough ammunition to ruin the entire family if he so chose.

Jonathon raised himself out of the leather chair. His joints were stiff from sitting, and his knees cracked in protest to the movement. He wrapped his arms around himself and vigorously rubbed each arm. Perhaps he should have allowed Chauncy to lay a fire.

He made his way to the fireplace and lit the oil lamp on the mantle. The room illuminated immediately, and Jonathon wished his life could be so easily lit.

A few unused logs remained in the hearth bin. Jonathon staggered them in the fireplace and kindled a small fire. As he warmed his hands, his eyes traveled to the portrait of his father. It was an old portrait, done soon after he had married. The image captured a radiance reflected in Peter Rexley's eyes that had been snuffed out long ago. Could his father have been so unhappily married that he would shame his wife by conceiving an illegitimate son? All evidence pointed to that end, yet the man had been devastated by his wife's death. It all did not make sense.

And what of Lark? Did Geoffry's parentage have anything to do with Peter Rexley's devotion to protecting her, saddling Jonathon with her?

The image of Lark rolled into his mind on a storm

cloud. Was there no end to this turmoil, to his father's secrets?

The cloud burst and rained terror and uncertainty. What if she and Geoffry were connected in some way? Perhaps that was the reason her life was in danger. Would revealing her identity put the boy's life in jeopardy also? Surely, his father would have disclosed such a thing. But evidently, there was much his father had seemed fit not to disclose.

Jonathon's stomach felt as if a wash maid had put it through the laundry wringer. His gaze fell and rested on the stack of condolence missives sent by friends and peers. He took them in his hand and made his way back to the desk.

As he sifted through them, he wondered how many of the people had actually known his father. How many had even set eyes on his father in the past decade. Peter Rexley had been shunned. It had been a constant struggle for Jonathon to retain the family dignity. Cyril was no help in that department. And friends? Well, there were very few of those. He had become so wary of everyone over the years. The members of the *ton* seemed so hypocritical in the way they had rejected his father that Jonathon had found it difficult to allow himself to trust anyone enough to make friends.

He read the next missive.

"To the bereaved family of Peter Rexley, Lord Somerset. Jonathon, it is with condolences I send this missive regarding the loss of your father. If there is anything I can do in your time of mourning, please do not hesitate. My condolences to Cyril and the balance of your kinsmen.

—Drew Hollingsworth"

"Now there is a friend," Jonathon announced to the empty room. Drew Hollingsworth. A friend no respected member of Society would claim, but a loyal friend nonetheless. Working for the London *Gazette* made the *ton* quite wary of Hollingsworth, but Jonathon found the news-writer to be much more constant than many a titled gent.

Jonathon tossed the missives onto the desk sending them sliding halfway across the heavily polished mahogany. Mulling in self-pity was accomplishing nothing, he decided forcefully.

He would contact Bentley Smythe first thing on the morrow, and he would find out more on this business with Aunt Harriet. That done, he would find some way to appease the biddy without engaging her thoughtless wrath. All he needed, on the brink of marrying a mute, while hiding that very woman in a wing of his own house, was Harriet parroting off like some angry bird.

He stormed to the doors with renewed conviction and flung them open. "Chauncy!"

The butler appeared out of nowhere. "You bellowed, my lord?"

Jonathon eyed Chauncy's bland expression and felt the tension drain from him. He smiled congenially. "Yes, Chauncy. I shall take some tea now, if you do not mind."

"Of course, my lord. Will you be joining the others or would you take your tea in your study."

"No, no. In my study. I think I have had enough of family for one day."

"I quite understand, m'lord," Chauncy turned precisely on his heel and made his way across the Great Room.

Chapter Six

A knock on the door stole Lark's breath. It was Lord Somerset. She had not seen him for almost a fortnight—the most harrowing two weeks in all her days. Lord Peter had lived alone, so once the few servants were retired or gone, the entire house had been hers to roam. But in these weeks since Lord Peter's death, Lark had been forced to remain silent all her doings, tiptoeing through the wing with the ease of a giraffe on the shells of eggs. She had not even been allowed to venture to the sanctuary of her peaceful library.

Jonathon entered, sharply dressed and ready for the day, a fact she could now describe in great detail. In the weeks they had been sequestered, Rebekka had coached Lark in the likes of fashion and other matters with which she would have to be flawless in order to enter Society. She had tried to tell her maid that she was serious when she had said she would not marry the brute, but Rebekka had worn them both ragged with all the reasons Lark would have to comply with Lord Peter's wishes. The most effective being the sacrifice he had made to ensure Lark's safety.

It was true, she did owe Lord Peter that, and so she had studied diligently. If she had to live the rest of her days with the new Lord Somerset, she wanted to at the very least, show him she would do all she could not to embarrass him.

Now, as he stood before her, all the hurt and anger he had dealt her swelled once more and eclipsed the affection she secretly held for him. She lifted herself gracefully off the chaise and forced a smile.

"I daresay your mathematical is the standard of precision and grace, Lord Somerset, and your Hussar boots are well kept." She graced him with a formal curtsy and waited while Rebekka translated what she had said with her hands. "But, I must remind you, I will still not become your wife." She hoped her knowledge would cut him to the quick for treating her like an imbecile.

Jonathon did not know whether to laugh or thrash the gel into submissiveness. As the abigail relayed his betrothed's words, he suddenly remembered a time when Lark was merely five. He and Cyril had been running in the fields on the Blackwell property, trying desperately to keep a kite in the air. Small Lark had wanted to help. A smile drew to Jonathon's lips as he remembered the haughty little sprite's reply to their denial of her wish.

"I must not only play with dolls! I can run and hold a string just as well as you, and if you do not take it back I shall tell Mama." She had pouted, her chubby face transforming into an almost perfect sphere. What an impudent little minx she had been.

Goodness! He had quite forgotten that. She could speak well enough then. What was the problem now? Had she been injured in the fire?

He studied her petulant expression, the way her eyes steeled with tenacity. Quite charming, really—in an odd sense. Still and all, he refused to be undermined by the likes of her. He would not be saddled with her if he could help it—and if he could not, well, he'd be damned if she would refuse him.

He turned and spoke to Rebekka. "Is there any way to communicate with her?"

Lark groaned and slumped back onto the chaise like a spoilt child who had just been told, no. Rebekka laughed, and Lark shot the abigail a scathing look.

"My lord, you must remember Lark can hear perfectly well. If you speak to her, she will respond."

Confound it! Of a certain, he had known she could hear—that was not quite what he had been asking.

Frustrated, he crossed the room in short order and came to stand above Lark. She lifted her gaze to him.

"I know you can hear me, Miss Blackwell. I meant; is there anyway at all I can learn to understand your replies. You seem to converse well enough with your abigail. You see," he motioned toward Rebekka, "it is quite irritating to have to rely on your abigail to translate your hand gestures."

Jonathon watched Lark's demeanor go from self-assurance to sadness. Her cornflower blue eyes, once sparkling, were suddenly crestfallen. What had he said?

She was doing it again, flinging fingers and hands in foreign gestures. He looked to Rebekka for guidance.

"Lark begs your forgiveness and asks if you might return another time. She is quite tired."

"She has not—" he stopped himself and drew his attention to Lark. "You have had leave of me for near a fortnight, yet you grow weary so soon? I trust our marriage will be a difficult matter for you to endure if my presence weakens you that much." He bowed politely and made his way to the door. "Rebekka, I would bid you come to the library when you have attended to Miss Blackwell." He quit the room without a further word to either of them.

Lark threw herself back on the chaise. "Oh he is heartless," she wailed with her hands. "He is so terribly, terribly awful. I shall never survive. Why did Lord Peter have to meet his demise?"

"Oh, nonsense, Miss Lark. You have never been overset by your arrangement in the past. Why begin this journey of self-pity now? You know very well that Lord Peter would not attach you to his son unless he thought it was a fine idea."

Rebekka came to kneel by Lark's side and took the younger girl's hand in her own. "Dear girl, could you not try to speak?" She asked softly. "It would be so much easier were you to talk to the lord with your own lips."

Lark viewed her abigail through tear-pooled eyes and shook her head slowly. How she wished she could speak, but no matter how much she desired it, conversing with Jonathon was not possible. Even if she did speak, he would never understand how she had come to rely on his father for so many years—indeed for the majority of her life. He would still think she was the conniving wench he'd called her that day in the library.

Rebekka patted Lark's hand. "All right, then. I must go to Lord Somerset. I advise you to be quiet until I return. I am quite sure the guests have gone since Lord Somerset made his appearance in these rooms, but I cannot be certain."

Lark nodded, knowing full well her dreadful role. She had spent her life in silent exile, and for all appearances, her situation was not going to change any time soon.

****

Jonathon stared at his mother's portrait. It had been such an age since he had resided in this house that it was rather comforting to be able to see her staring back at him on a daily basis. She was smiling on him in the dainty way he remembered of old—quite comforting, indeed. What would she think of his father's odd behavior? And of this new development?

Perhaps he would have some answers once he spoke with Bentley Smythe. Jonathon had attempted to contact the solicitor, but his business associate had said he was away on some family errand. It had quite perturbed Jonathon. However, the past fortnight had kept him occupied with family and grieving, and now it would not be too much longer before Smythe was at his disposal. Presently, Jonathon's most pressing concern was Lark.

He sat on the settee and drew a long taste of the claret he'd poured himself. How was he going to introduce Lark into society without the entire *ton* prattling to one another about her sudden presence? He could hear the chatty questions already. "From where does she hail?" "How did you make her acquaintance?"

Well, he had six months of mourning to discover the answers to those forthcoming questions.

The library doors slid open, and Rebekka stepped in. Jonathon rose to his feet. "There you are. Come in, come in," he said.

Rebekka approached and bobbed a cordial curtsy. "You wished to see me, m'lord."

He bestowed on her what he hoped was a reassuring smile. "Do sit down, Rebekka. I do not mean to sound the ogre. I am merely overtired."

"I think no such thing of you, m'lord," Rebekka told him as she perched like a nervous sparrow on the edge of a gilt chair.

"I wish to know about Miss Lark. We must be sure she is ready to make an appearance in society." Jonathon began to pace the floor. He felt like a caged animal, knowing not whether the cage was a sanctuary or a prison. Silently he cursed his father for putting him in this predicament. He stopped and turned to face Rebekka. "With her inability to speak, she shall have to be impeccable in every other respect in order to escape the gossipmongers."

"Yes, m'lord. There has not been any need to worry about the social graces until now, but I assure you, I have been coaching her this fortnight past."

"Miss Lark seems to have many social graces. That is not to what I refer. She must be apprised of the latest fashions, *on-dits* that every acceptable young miss must know."

"I quite comprehend m'lord. Lark is a bright gel. Had no choice really, what with only books and me for company. But her brain is sharp. She learns quickly."

"I suppose she knows nothing of dance?" He sipped his claret.

"No, I would daresay Miss Lark knows nothing of dance and it is unfortunate that I do not possess that knowledge or skill myself. I cannot instruct her."

He lifted his hand in deference. "It is of little consequence. I may not enjoy the activity, but I am accomplished enough to teach her, I suppose."

"I am sure Miss Lark would be most grateful. She does so want to please you, m'lord." Rebekka's cryptic smile held something unbeknownst, yet intriguing.

"Does she? She did not bestow an enthusiastic reception on me when I arrived at her chambers earlier. She would rather this entire wedding be forgotten, would she not?"

"No, m'lord, I assure you. It is best difficult for Miss Lark to believe you are willing to take her to wife when you haven't seen her this past decade." Rebekka smiled confidently. "Lord Peter said you were a willing husband." She lowered her eyes the smile barely fading from her lips. "I must confess, even I did not understand how you could hold regard for Lark when you thought she no longer lived. Still and all, it was a surprise to us both when you seemed put off by the idea. If I may be so bold, did you not wish the marriage, my lord?"

Jonathon tried to appear relaxed, although the maid's question rankled him. It was outside of enough have to comply with things thrust upon him. Questions were going to be leveled by Society to which he had no answers, and now he was questioned even by the hired help. Still, he needed information from her, and so had to appear as if he were completely aware. "I don't know why you would view me as 'put off'. What exactly did my father say to Miss Lark?" He asked carefully, not wanting to alert Rebekka to his prying mind. One who thought they were discussing mutually shared knowledge often sang a much prettier song than one who thought they were divulging secret information. "What exactly did my father say to Miss Lark?"

Confusion marred Rebekka's countenance for a moment. "He said you had always held a fondness for Miss Lark." Her brows came together in worry. "Is that not so, m'lord?"

"Did it not occur to Miss Lark that I had not seen her since she was a mere child?"

"Of course, m'lord, but Lord Peter informed Miss Lark that he had discussed her with you after your illness some time past and that you had quite fallen for her quiet disposition and willingness to please. Being aware of the manner which Lord Peter could tell a tale, it did not seem so farfetched that he could tell you of Miss Lark's true disposition in a way that would win your heart."

Yes, Peter Rexley certainly was good at spinning a yarn—whether the story be true or not. Without doubt, the man could've sold London Bridge to the Americans— indeed, to someone with no water to cross for miles. His father had been quite convincing in days gone by— perhaps unto his end, Jonathon considered, now that he knew his father was not as insane as everyone believed, but evidently, a great deal more conniving.

"One more thing, and then I will allow you to return to attending Miss Lark. What say you about this hand language of hers? Is it something easily learned?"

"Are you asking if I could teach it to you, m'lord?"

He nodded, and a grin that would stretch across the Thames blossomed on her face. "'Twould be considerably easier for me to converse with my wife if we spoke the same language, would it not?"

"Oh, indeed, m'lord," the abigail answered, a curious

glow in her deep brown eyes. "There is but one complication. You see, the language she speaks is French."

"What do you mean? She understands when we speak to her, does she not?"

Rebekka nodded. "The fellow who developed it, well, he developed it for French." She laughed. "I had a time with the language myself when first Lord Peter had sent me to study. But my lady, she took to French as if it were her natural tongue—the hand language, too, for that matter."

Jonathon was thoroughly intrigued. A woman who could not utter a sound actually understood two languages. Quite fascinating. "You mean to tell me, you not only translate her hand language to the spoken word, you also translate French into English?"

Rebekka let out a giggle. "'Tis not as difficult as it sounds."

"And there is no way for her to make the signs in the English language?"

"Not that I know of, my lord. In order to understand her hand signs, you must know French."

Fascinating, Jonathon thought. "Not to worry. I am quite fluent in French. It should not be a hindrance," he told the abigail.

Rebekka stood, clapping her hands together like an excited child. "Oh, Miss Lark will be so pleased!"

"Tell Miss Lark nothing," Jonathon ordered. He was preparing for the worst, but still planned to find a way out of this charade.

Chapter Seven

Lark spied herself in the looking glass, tilting her head this way then that, trying to decide if the angouleme suited her. The bonnet's fluted crown caused her face to appear too long, she decided with a frown, but the extensive broad brim would shield her from the sun nicely.

Sun, what a delightful word, that. Soon she would be able to enjoy sunlight without fear of discovery, without a time ration looming over her like some ominous, unbearable death warrant. What would it be like to stroll through a park on the arm of Lord Somerset? Her handsome lord would turn the heads of many ladies, Lark was sure, and despite the conflict that warred within her, she would be served a platter of pride to be seen with him.

She was a ninny, in love with a man who offended her every feeling, a man who considered her a disgrace, a man who would never return her love.

She removed the bonnet and returned it carefully to its place, her mind overfull of the image of Lord Somerset. Her childish romantic ideas had imbedded themselves so deeply within, she could not bring herself to remain angry with him. To the contrary, she sympathized with his situation—regardless of what Lord Peter had said, this marriage had obviously been sprung on Jonathon. It shredded her pride, and tore her heart, to know that he held her in such contempt, would feel no pride bubble within him at the image of her by his side. If only she could bring herself to speak. If only she could prove to him her worth. But how could she accomplish such a task when she was unsure of her own merit?

A seed of uneasiness sprouted in her stomach.

She had so much to learn in so little time. She was positive she would make a mistake in the midst of the *ton* and bring dishonor to her betrothed. That knowledge weighed heavy in the middle of her stomach.

The door opened and Rebekka entered with a huge smile brightening her face. Lark frowned. "Why do you return in such a mood?"

Rebekka gave the lady a shrug. "I am happy for you, Miss Lark. Your betrothal will be a great event."

"Nonsense," Lark protested, her stiff fingers emphasizing her uneasiness. "'Twill be disastrous. I am sure to shame the poor man in public and he already believes my brain to be as deficient as my voice. I am sure to do something to confirm his suspicions."

Rebekka's eyes glowed as if she possessed a secret. "I fear you are to be surprised by his lordship, Miss Lark. Find patience and you will be rewarded. Of that I would stake the world."

"A worthless wager," Lark protested, "since the world is not yours to mortgage." She relaxed in a gilt chair and began to make a note in her journal.

A rapping came at the chamber door. Lark froze, her thoughts in unexpected turmoil. She motioned for Rebekka to open the door. Jonathon stepped across the threshold with such ease and presence that it seemed he had crossed under that lintel on a regular basis.

Lark rose to greet him, but he spoke before she could scarce raise a finger.

"I would you take dinner with me this evening, Miss Lark. It seems if we are to wed, we should become acquainted with one another." His booming tone was authoritative, almost demanding. "Rebekka will escort you down the rear stairwell and around to the front door. This way all suspicion will be avoided." He bowed politely and left, leaving Lark standing with her mouth fallen open.

She stared at the closed portal before snapping her mouth shut. She wasn't sure he could practice any manners at all. How could she have fallen for such a thoughtless man? She let out a grunt. "He is pomposity itself," she signed.

"Aye," Rebekka agreed, "but such a handsome fellow." She turned her back on her charge and opened the carved mahogany doors of the wardrobe. "We had better be sure you look your best tonight."

Lark would have liked to comment a few choice words, but Rebekka refused to turn around to receive them. In a disconcerted frump, Lark sat in the chair and allowed Rebekka to pick out the evening's dinner attire.

A short time later, Lark gave Chauncy a demure smile when he greeted her and Rebekka at the front door. What must he think of this situation? He and Penelope, his wife and Chief of the Kitchen, knew about her living arrangements. He must think it awfully strange to be summoned to the door by Lark herself.

"Ladies," he said quite politely. "Do come in. Lord Somerset has instructed me to show you directly into the dining room." He escorted them into the dining room as if Lark were as important as the Prince Regent himself then bowed out.

The room was aglow from the sconces on the decorated walls, the table illuminated by two silver candelabra that revealed the most delicately decorated china—small pink roses encircled by a band of gold. Crystal wine glasses, three to be exact, frosted with etched roses graced the place settings.

Lark glanced at Rebekka then back to the table. She had taken meals in this room several times over the years, but never had it appeared so elegant. While Lord Peter was not exactly the eccentric most had thought him to be, he genuinely did not go for show, either.

He had lost his zeal for life after the death of his wife and of that, Lark could sympathize to the full. Although only a child when the fire claimed the lives of all but a few of those she loved, she had felt the loss with the heart of an adult. Perhaps more so, for through these many years there had been something—a touch of doubt, perhaps fear?—that had chipped away at her consciousness. A feeling deep inside, almost tangible, yet elusive that hinted of an understanding of what had happened that fateful night. There were times she strove at remembrance, hopeful her secretive mind might know something that could free her from the guilt of having been the only survivor of that house—save Rebekka, of course.

Penelope came into the room with a platter of something hidden beneath a dome of silver. Her graying hair was neatly capped, her blue dress covered by a protective white apron. Lark smiled at her warmly.

"Good evening, Miss Lark," Penelope said in her thick southwestern brogue. "I trust you an' 'is Lordship will 'ave a fine sooppa."

"A fine supper, indeed, if you have done the making," Lark said with her hands and waited for Rebekka to translate the reply.

"Ah, sooch a lovely gel, y'are," Penelope replied with sincere admiration. "Naught a farthing of pretentiousness in ye."

"I see all is prepared on schedule."

Lark spun at Jonathon's voice resonating directly behind her. He appeared a touch startled by her sudden movement, then his dark eyes softened and he reached a hand out, although he did not actually touch her. "I did not mean to frighten you, my dear. Please accept my humble apology." He took her hand and bowed over it.

Dear. The sentiment resounded in Lark's mind evoking a wonderfully joyous resonance. Perhaps he would come to realize she was not to blame for this betrothal and would treat her kindly.

She gave him a hopeful smile and signed.

"Miss Lark says she looks forward to the evening meal with you, my lord," Rebekka translated.

He proffered his crooked arm. "Shall we dine?"

She showed him a polite smile then slipped her arm into his. The warmth of his essence penetrated his dark brown velvet coat sleeve and extended itself to Lark. She closed her eyes as it traveled through every nerve in her body, wrapping her in a warmth replete with comfort and hope. She forced the corners of her mouth to remain in a constant line, lest he realize her response to his touch. She needed to be indifferent to him, but her emotions refused to cooperate with her head. He was marrying her only out of obligation and respect for his father's dying wish. The best she could hope for was a cordial friendship that would make both their lives tolerable. Regardless of how much she secretly wished otherwise, she had to remember that.

She had to.

With a word to Rebekka to join them, he escorted

Lark to the table and offered her a chair, then sat at the head of the table to her left. Noticing Rebekka still loitering by the entrance, he turned his attention to the abigail. "Please join us, Rebekka," he said.

"But my lord—"

"Please do not argue, Rebekka. There is already a place set for you. Don't waste time while our supper proves ready to be served."

Rebekka inclined her head and took her place opposite her charge. Lark smiled reassurance at her abigail in an odd exchange of roles.

Penelope entered the dining room and served a delightful dinner of lamb, roast potatoes, and an array of vegetables as pleasing to the eye as to the palate. Lark sat in awe as the delectable aroma filled the room, a combination of sweet cherries and unknown spices. She politely commended the meal to Lord Somerset, and he replied in stiff monotones between bites. She found her earlier hope snuffed out quite effectively. If this foreshadowed the meals they would take together once they were wed, companionship was definitely missing. Lark once again doubted the sanity in Peter Rexley's entire scheme.

As Penelope removed the soiled supper plates, Jonathon turned his attention to Rebekka. "I trust you have enjoyed the meal?" She looked puzzled for a moment, gazing at Lark as if awaiting a reply. "I was asking you, Rebekka, not Miss Lark. I have, of a certain, learned to address her directly by now."

Rebekka nodded slowly. "Yes, my lord. The meal was delicious, and you are most kind."

"And a dead bore," Lark added with her hands. Rebekka must have caught the rebuke out of the corner of her eye, for she threw Lark a scathing reprimand.

"What did she say?" Jonathon asked Rebekka.

Rebekka faltered only for a moment before replying. "She added her opinion of the evening, my lord," she replied evenly.

Jonathon eyed Lark for a time. He felt like the odd one out of a joke, and he didn't know whether to be insulted or utterly incensed. He was most definitely going to have to learn this hand-language; otherwise, she might cut him to the quick at every turn and leap. Besides, there were truths his father had omitted regarding Lark and the Blackwell estate, and if he were going to uncover what was presently well-concealed, he was going to have to understand everything his pretty intended was saying.

Thoughts charged through his head. She was so beautiful and polite it was difficult to imagine her being part of some sort of elaborate hoax and judging by what Rebekka had said about his father, Lark seemed innocent. But what if that were not the case? What if she were actually shrewd enough to make anyone fall for her charade? He certainly did not want to find himself duped. Or even worse, in a grave situation which jeopardized lives.

Lark's face grew cold as the blood retreated. Jonathon sat at her side, staring at her with the most horrified expression ever to be directed at her. She found herself both wanting to know what was going on in his mind and fearing that very thing as well.

He wrenched his gaze from hers and turned to Rebekka. "You may retire for the evening."

Lark's heart ceased to beat. She shook her head, her fingers moving in a frenzied flurry.

"It is all right," Rebekka said in a soothing tone before addressing Lord Somerset. "Miss Lark would prefer I stay if it is acceptable to you, my lord. She wonders how you both would communicate without my interpreting for you."

Jonathon turned a steady gaze to Lark. "I am sure we can manage to communicate somehow. You need not worry."

Lark was unsure whom he was trying to encourage. Her own mind was certainly not set at ease. She spoke again with her hands.

"My lady wishes to remind you of etiquette, my lord. If anyone were to discover you had been together without benefit of a chaperon..."

He raised a silencing finger. "Do not preach to me about protocol. Our situation is not only highly unusual, but exceeds all need for the worry of etiquette, don't you agree? We are residing in the same house without benefit of marriage. I think that situation is a trifle more volatile than taking an unchaperoned conversation in the confines of the dining room. Why, should the peers discover our situation, we wouldn't have to worry about entertaining at all, for we would both be reduced to the scathed of society."

Although she desperately wished it, Lark could not think of another argument. She knew little of the goings on in the *ton*, but she did know how cruel they could be. Lord Peter had made it clear to her time and again how important it was to follow the peerage's example. It was one of the many reasons she was so paralyzed by the thought of entering society without the use of her tongue.

Not for the first time since Lord Peter's death, Lark reasoned that she should able herself to speak. Her throat constricted with the thought, and breathing became difficult as apprehension balled inside her. She lowered her gaze and willed herself to calm.

When she raised her head once again, she found Jonathon eyeing her with the oddest expression. Lark could not discern if he were upset, angry or concerned. She moved her attention to Rebekka.

"You can retire. I suppose we'll weather fairly," Lark signed to her abigail.

"That's my girl," Rebekka signed back. "I shall excuse myself, then," she said aloud, then got up and politely nodded. "Miss Lark, my lord."

Lark and Jonathon watched in silence as Rebekka quit the room then he smiled at his fiancée. He watched the sparks ignite in her lovely expressive eyes and knew he had irritated her once again. Despite himself, he thought she was delightful. "Would you mind repeating that," he inquired blandly, when he realized she was doing that thing with her hands, knowing full well he would not understand.

She got up, rang the bell and began to pace the room. After a moment, Chauncy came in.

"You rang, my lord," he drolled.

Jonathon let out a chuckle. "Not I, Chauncy, Miss Lark."

Chauncy directed the most mannerly of smiles to the young miss. "What service may I provide, Miss?"

Lark motioned with her hands in a gesture that

resembled writing then studied Chauncy with query in her eyes.

"You wish a tablet and quill?"

She nodded, and Chauncy bowed out of the room, returning in no time with a tablet, ink and quill. He placed them on the table in front of her and she bestowed on him the most grateful of smiles. "Thank you," she signed.

"You are very welcome, my lady. Is there anything else?" He moved his attention to Jonathon. "My lord?"

Jonathon quashed the urge to laugh at Chauncy. In all his memories, there wasn't one of the manservant getting in such a pother over anybody. Why, the butler was downright coddling Lark and, by Jove—the bloody hoyden—preened as if she were one of those ninnyhammer come-out gels.

"That will be all, Chauncy."

"Very good, my lord." As the butler backed away, Jonathon thought he saw the corners of Chauncy's mouth twitch.

Jonathon turned his attention to Lark, who sat writing furiously. She looked up and shoved the tablet at him with a force that should have shattered his image of her ethereal innocence. Perhaps it would have, had it not been for the unguarded insecurity in her blue eyes.

He took the paper and read, "I find it highly unconscionable, my lord, that you would compromise my position in this manner. Perhaps it would be best if we forgot the entire betrothal. I am sure, with Rebekka's aid, I can find a position somewhere, perhaps a husband."

"You think I would jeopardize everything because of a silly affront you feel at being left alone in a room with me? You must consider me a scatterbrained idiot!"

Lark snatched the tablet from him and scribbled once again. "I understand that this situation must be a best difficult for you. It is quite unbearable for me also. But we cannot allow Lord Peter to dictate our future. A future that will be clouded for you being wed to a woman for whom you hold such high contempt. Besides, I might do quite well to leave this house after such a time."

"Is that what you want? To leave this house?" The reaction his body had to that was a thing he had not before experienced and could therefore not label. A mixture of anger and—despair?—and frustration. Whatever the combination, anger rose to the surface and made itself unmistakably known. He shot out of the chair. "You may as well put away silly notions, Miss Lark. You are to be my wife, and you will live in this house the rest of your life. I suggest you get very well acquainted with that fact; else, life will be exceedingly difficult for you. I plan to follow my father's instructions to the letter. Is that clear?"

"Quite clear, my lord," she signed, evidentially forgetting he could not understand. She bolted out of the chair and ran from the room.

Chapter Eight

The library was cold. Jonathon had allowed the fire to ebb into orange-edged cinders. Without really seeing them, he sat watching the shadows dance across his mother's portrait. His feelings for his betrothed were so unsteady, scant was his ability to understand them. Because she was so willing to go on her way with nothing, he now felt without doubt that Lark was innocent of scheming, but the possibility that she might be connected to Geoffry, and might put that young lad's life at risk, still plagued him. He needed Smythe's report on all of his father's secrets—and soon. He sipped the sherry he had poured.

He shouldn't have been so rough on her, broken her spirit. She was not only furious when she had taken her leave of him, but had been on the brink of shedding tears. He should have been kinder, but he'd been so out of sorts since his father's wishes had been made known to him, he had not once considered that Lark might actually *wish* to leave Somerset Manor, and her pronouncement had sent him reeling.

His reaction had kept him at odds with himself these hours past. He wanted her to stay; he wanted her to leave—nay, he wanted her to be normal so that wanting her would be acceptable.

Damnation! He didn't know what he wanted.

A loud commotion out of doors arrested his thoughts, and he made his way into the great room with a hastened step. Chauncy, donned in a dressing gown and nightcap, staggered out with sleep-hazed eyes.

"Go back to your chamber, Chauncy. I shall deal with this myself."

Chauncy bade him a groggy good night then disappeared once again. Jonathon unlatched the door, thrusting it open with such a force as to startle his unwelcome guest.

"Cyril! What the devil are you doing, calling at such an unholy hour?"

Cyril pushed past his brother and stumbled into the great room.

"You're foxed," Jonathon observed with disgust.

"Not quite," Cyril remarked, "merely a little espirited." He straightened his spine. "Suppose you don't have time for your brother now that you're lord of the manor, eh, old chum? Thought perhaps you were turning into Papa, what with your absence out and about."

"Balderdash." Jonathon waved away his brother's ranting. "So my mourning is not up to standard. What of it? Before the cock crows, I shall have a wife to consider. But I suppose responsibility is a word with which you are unfamiliar." He returned to his glass of sherry in the library without thought to his brother.

Cyril followed not at all contrite at his disruption. "In case you hadn't noticed, brother, I am quite in mourning myself."

"I see your mourning. Making the rounds once again at Ascot and White's, and no doubt every other club has seen the benefit of your company?"

"I don't know that I would call it benefit." Cyril helped himself to a glass of brandy.

Jonathon expelled a deep breath. "What brings you here?"

"Not happy for the pleasure of my company?" Coming from someone else the remark may have sounded caustic, but Cyril had a way with lightening his derision. Nonetheless, Jonathon was not in the mood for bantering with his brother. The hour was late and he was growing quickly weary.

"Surprised to be precise."

"Of course surprised."

"Why should I expect your hasty return? A fortnight ago, you weren't happy to be in this house once again. As I recall, you didn't find advantage in attending the reading of the Will, you held our papa with such disregard."

Cyril's eyes darkened as he viewed his brother with an intensity that made Jonathon uncomfortable. "Does it

59

not bother you, Jon, that he turned us out and subsequently turned up his toes without so much as an explanation?"

Jonathon's irritation dissolved; for the first time he understood his brother's dilemma. For himself, his father's actions were all explained. The letter the man left had made clear so much of his odd behavior that Jonathon no longer felt any residual hostility, but Cyril did not have the benefit of reading that letter, or of understanding the need for their father's odd behavior in years past—And Jonathon could not enlighten him now.

"I hold no animosity towards the man," he told his Cyril. "Had I the time perhaps it would be well worth dwelling on his oddities, however, I quite choose to overlook the subject."

"Then you are a better son than I, brother." Cyril turned up the bottom on his glass and drained the contents. "Don't suppose you would allow me to stay until the morrow?" He shook his head with haste. "No. Never mind," he mumbled.

Jonathon was at odds with himself, unsure as to whether he should give Cyril a bed for the night, or not. Despite Cyril's genuine case of the doldrums, Jonathon could not afford the expense of having Cyril find out about Lark. Jonathon could well envisage his brother inadvertently telling everything while well into his cups. Still he did not know how to turn Cyril out without feeling guilty himself.

For several moments, he sat in silence sipping his spirits and contemplating how to dismiss Cyril without stirring up suspicion or ire. He placed his glass on the mantle, glancing at his mother's portrait for but a moment. "Would it not be best for you to return home this eve?" He asked at length with a hope he didn't sound as tinny to Cyril as he did to his own ears.

"Acting Lord Somerset, ay, Jon? Turning me out and hibernating behind these walls. You know the gossipmongers are having their fill."

"I don't give a farthing for the vacuous prattle boxes. I have well addressed that accusation before and shall not entertain it again. Yes, I am Lord Somerset now, no I am not in hiding; I am in quiet mourning. I merely choose not to make an event of my sorrow as is *á la modalité*. Never you mind, in a trice all will see me merrily introducing my betrothed." Jonathon was not sure why he engaged in the useless conversation with his inebriated brother, except maybe that he had felt quite closed-in himself of late.

He had never wished to live in the shadow of his father's oddities, and did not really care to do so now, but that was going to be quite impossible with a deficient wife in tow.

"How is Miss Blackburn, by the way?" Cyril refilled his empty glass, missing the askance look Jonathon directed at him.

"She is well enough," Lord Somerset replied in short.

"Such a lovely thing. I daresay you are quite in the pink to have found her. Pity she fails to speak, though. That will surely set the tongues to wagging." Cyril laughed at his weak pun, staggered backward, and fell into a chair.

"Must we discuss this now, Cyril?" Jonathon asked testily. "You arrive unannounced, well into your cups, and wish to discuss the inadequacy of my fiancée, all at an ungodly hour. When will you learn you are no longer in short coats and should act accordingly?" Jonathon made his way to the doors and flung them open. "I am retiring. I suggest you do the same." He began to quit the room but Cyril's retort stopped him.

"Sounds as if her failing is a bother to you. If you truly loved her, would you not be more indifferent?"

Jonathon spun on the heel of his Hussars. His blood coursed though his veins heating every part of him. It throbbed in his temple, in his neck; his heart beat quickening. "You are out of yourself, Cyril and I strongly suggest you remember your place. You will not speak ill of my betrothed. You will not speak ill of my intentions, and you most certainly will not insinuate, even in the slightest, that all is not the picture of heaven between us. Do I make myself clear?" All he needed was for Cyril to begin a personal investigation into the life of Lark and how she had come to be betrothed. Cyril might be a wastrel, but a cork brain he was not—and he enjoyed solving a mystery as much as the next fellow.

Cyril's face was blank for quite some time, as if he

could not believe Jonathon's intense wrath. At length he pulled himself out of the chair, crossed the room and placed a hand on Jonathon's shoulder. "Calm yourself, brother. I meant nothing by the gibe. Are we not brothers able to tease one another?"

Jonathon's rage quickly ebbed. He knew Cyril meant him no ill. Regretful of his outburst, he eased out from underneath his brother's warm hand.

"I take no offense. It is only that the hour grows late and I am weary. Why don't you retire to your room and we'll breakfast on the morrow before you depart."

Cyril nodded and together the brothers climbed the stairs. "Gammon!" Jonathon bit out when they reached the landing. Cyril turned an inquiring eye towards his brother.

"You go on without me. I quite forgot something." Jonathon turned before Cyril could say more than a quizzical "something?"

At a concealed spot halfway down the staircase, Jonathon waited for his brother's footfalls to fade before returning to the landing and going the opposite direction down the corridor. His hand was raised to rap on the door to Lark's chamber when he heard footfalls once again.

In the shadows, he lurked until he could see but the outline of Cyril descending the staircase. Jonathon's arm relaxed without having touched the door. With haste, he made his way to the apex of the stairs. "Looking for me?"

Hand over his heart Cyril abruptly turned on the second-to-last step. He looked as if he would alight right out of his boots." You quite scared me into the grave," he said breathlessly. "You are a magician to have climbed above without notice."

"No magician, Cyril. You seemed rather intent on descending the stairs with little thought to anything else. Why might that be?"

Cyril ignored his brother's gruff questioning and drew his lips into an unaffected smile. "I merely thought perhaps you might need some assistance with the 'something' you forgot," Cyril answered.

"I am finished. I thank you for your consideration. Shall we retire?"

Blast it all! How was he going to alert Lark to Cyril's

presence now?

Chapter Nine

Lark sat in the gazebo watching a sparrow peck at the minute specks on the ground. It looked as though the bird sought food in vain, but still it pecked and flew into the nearby tree, then returned again and again to the same spot.

She smiled and noted the airy breeze in her journal. She loved mornings out on the grounds. She sipped on the piping tea Penelope had brought her. Last evening had been a trial, but the brightness of the new day seemed to overshadow past tribulations.

In the light of morning, she resigned herself to the reality of her powerlessness to stop the betrothal, and her powerlessness to make Lord Somerset care for her. Even if she were able to speak, he would not love her. His low opinion of her obviously went beyond her inability to converse.

Unfortunately, her heart—a heart that had not really belonged to her for an age—refused to be comforted by mere resignation. That was why she had offered to leave. She did not think she could spend the rest of her life loving him knowing he loathed her...Yet there had been moments when she thought she saw glimpses of admiration in his gaze.

Oh, what had Lord Peter done? Confusion filled her soul.

Footfalls nearing the gazebo alerted Lark to someone's approach. A part of her wished it were Jonathon for she had not seen him all morning and hoped to mend the rift, but another part of her was afraid of that inevitable confrontation. She adjusted her pale blue day dress and twisted to peer through the white braided slats of the gazebo.

To her surprise, it was neither Jonathon nor Rebekka, but Mister Cyril Rexley. Her mind started to whir with possible excuses for her presence at the manor at such an inappropriately early hour—and without the company of her betrothed and a chaperon.

"I thought it was you out here on this fine morning, Miss Lark," Cyril said as he stepped into the gazebo.

Lark smiled and was glad of her silent state for the first time in many days.

"Do you mind if I sit and enjoy the pleasure of your company for a time?" Cyril bowed politely and waited for Lark to nod before sitting an appropriate distance from her. "I see you are writing. Am I to assume, then, that we might converse by such means?"

Lark studied her future brother-in-law. He did not seem to find it strange, her presence this morning. No accusation showed in his amused eyes and none laced his tone. She wondered if he was merely shielding his suspicions or if he truly saw nothing amiss. She nodded and removed a fresh page to begin the conversation. A fluttering of nerves jostled her stomach. She had to be careful not to give away her living arrangements.

"What is that you are writing?" Cyril motioned to her pages.

"Nothing of importance, Sir. I enjoy recording my thoughts at times," she wrote.

He read her response and then eyed her with a scrutiny that worried her. "You are highly unusual, miss. Not so much that you would record your thought, mind you. I daresay many a woman does that, but rather that you would so openly admit the fact. What were I, or anyone else for that matter, to take and read of it?"

Lark clutched her words firmly. Never had she thought that someone else might partake of her journal. There were private thoughts recorded within, but no one in the household would dare to invade.

"I would not dare to do such a thing, of course," he assured her. "I merely wondered at the possibility. I have not met a lady with so open and honest a response ere this day. Forgive me if I offended you."

"You did not offend, Sir. I was but surprised."

"That was of the obvious," Cyril replied to her written rebuttal.

"Your tongue is quite frank."

He chuckled, then. "Forgive my insolence if you deem it such, I have never been overblessed with manners."

Lark considered Mister Rexley for some time. It was true he spoke words that seemed to raise the hackles of many, but she could not help but to like him. There was an honesty in his lack of tact that seemed much more virtuous than the backhanded niceties exuded from the likes of, say, Lady Wescotte.

Besides, she saw something of her own situation in the likes of Cyril Rexley. He was of a respected family, but still not quite accepted by the ripened fruit of society. She would be the same.

Her gaze met Cyril's and she graced him with a smile ornate with kindness and gratitude. "I must say, Mr. Rexley, I think I am going to like you."

If only Jonathon would see her in such unclouded regard as did his brother. Perhaps then . . .

As if manifested by her own thoughts, Jonathon suddenly appeared on the gazebo.

"Good morning, Miss Lark. Cyril." His words were as cordial as could be on a beautiful morning such as this, but Lark noted how the scowl furrowing his brow belied the tranquility of his greeting.

"I do hope my brother hasn't been bothering you, Miss Lark," he said with a reproachful glance at his sibling.

Lark smiled and shook her head carefully. She did not understand the manner in which Jonathon's jaw clenched so tightly. It was a wonder he could even speak considering just how little his mouth actually opened.

"My dear brother, I was merely keeping the miss company. No need to draw your dagger." Cyril stood and clapped his brother on the back. "I daresay you are a lucky man, though."

"I am sure you don't mean to insult my future wife, so I will take that remark as a compliment of my judgment rather than an assessment of some seedy time you have spent together."

Lark's gasp had both men turning their attention to her. She wrote furiously upon her paper, then stood and shoved it under Lord Somerset's nose. "You insult me yourself, sir. If you think me undignified, perhaps you should find another to wed."

Cyril chuckled as he craned his neck to read Lark's words. "Guess she told you, old chap. You did slip into a 'Cyril' mode there for a time. Question my motives all you want to, brother, but fair your maiden well. She did not invite me to join her; I came upon her quite by accident."

Jonathon knew he had gone too far. He had not meant to hurt or insult her, he had just been so furious when he witnessed her smiling at Cyril. A smile so sweet and encompassing should have been meant only for...him—and the way Cyril gazed at her, well, that was downright reprehensible. A seed that much resembled jealousy had sprouted in his stomach when he entered the gardens and took note of their warm and friendly exchange. He might not be able to have Lark, but the idea of someone else wooing her curdled the blood in his veins.

"Besides, Jon, if you truly care for this lady's reputation, you wouldn't have her here at such an hour without chaperon." Cyril's chide sounded much like a deliberate taunt. "At least when there are guests in the house to find you out," he added, the corners of his mouth twitching.

Jonathon wanted to throttle his brother.

"If I am not mistaken I invited no guests to spend last evening. They quite invited themselves by arriving in such a state as they could not possibly find the door back out into the cold." He felt the nerve twitch in his jaw. Maintaining control was an arduous task.

Cyril, with apparently no control left whatsoever, burst into a million laughs. Jonathon ignored him and turned to Lark. Her unsure eyes darted from one brother to the next.

Jonathon took a step towards her and effectively shut Cyril out of the conversation. With a gentle hand, he lowered Lark's outstretched arm that still held her rebuke to his face. He took her arm in his and looked at her in earnest.

"I apologize for insulting you. I was not thinking. I was out of my mind with worry when I saw you with Cyril. I thought..." What was he doing? He cut himself off and rethought what he was about to say. To utter the words he had, but in the nick of time swallowed, would

Nicola Beaumont

only serve to either insult her once again or scare her from him entirely. He wanted to accomplish neither. She had his emotions quite in a tizzy—one minute vexing him, the next charming him out of his boots. She was like a child, really. He looked on her and amended that thought. No child was she. Sheltered, perhaps, but no child—not in body or in temperament.

He glanced down at her hand laying in his, his gaze traveling up her gloved arm. His heart almost stopped its steady beat when he noticed a blemish unhidden where the top of her glove met her alabaster skin. "What is that?" he demanded, dropping her hand.

She glanced at the mark on her arm, her face startled and flush. She shook her head and bolted past both Jonathon and Cyril.

"Blast!" Jonathon bit out. That crescent-shaped blemish was the very same as the one as on his own papa's shoulder.

68

Chapter Ten

Air refused to fill Jonathon's lungs. Reality tunneled; everything around him disappeared until all that remained was the mirror image of his father's birthmark on Lark's arm. It screamed unholy possibilities. His father had produced one illegitimate child. Why not two? Could this be the reason Peter Rexley had been so secretive and adamant about Lark's identity and whereabouts? Surely, his father would not have betrothed him to his own half-sister. But how could he be sure? Had not his father's letter referred to Lark "as a sister" and had it not instructed Jonathon to a marriage of convenience only?

No, he could not believe his father would do such a thing, yet mot a year ago, he would have never believed Peter Rexley could commit adultery, but Aunt Harriet had legal papers proving that disability.

His mind's eye traveled up Lark's arm and rested on her lovely face. So innocent, so inviting. Absently, he smiled at the way her mouth pouted when she was angry—the way she slumped in her chair, or stormed off, when he damaged her sensibilities. He did not realize until this very moment that losing her would be so painful. His growing feelings for her made his heart hurt. And now, to discover the possibility that she might be forever off-limits was unbearable. He needed desperately to speak with Bentley Smythe.

"Jon?" Cyril's hand touched Jonathon's shoulder; reality came crashing to the fore, as he remembered the intimate rendezvous Lark and Cyril had shared.

Jonathon spun to face his brother. "How dare you take private audience with her." The words blasted from his mouth, and Cyril's playful countenance did nothing to alleviate Jonathon's black mood.

"I daresay you are bitten by that proverbial monster

69

who dons the color green." Cyril grinned at his brother in a way very familiar and very irritating.

"Poppycock! Jealousy has absolutely nothing to do with my reaction, brother mine. You are incorrigible, compromising the family's reputation, but more importantly, that of Miss Lark. What were people to find out about your private interlude? She would be labeled a light skirt in no time. Did you think not of that?" Jonathon groaned in disgust. "Selfish, Cyril, that's what you are. Always have been, always shall be."

"You wound me. A shade knavish, perhaps, but never, *never* selfish. Why, I am constantly of the mind of others. To let the truth be known, it was my utter concern for your fiancée that led me to be in her company from the start." Cyril gave a practiced flip to his coattail and sat, peering up into his brother's eyes in quite apparent anticipation.

Jonathon expelled a long sigh that proved to animate his frustration, and cause his brother's lips to curve into that irritating, upturned state once again. Cyril sat, crossed one leg over the other, and draped a lazy arm across the back of the seat cushion.

"I haven't seen you in such an agitated state since Papa ousted us from this very house. I daresay it's quite refreshing to see you still have some emotion, brother."

"I suppose I have 'nodcock' printed across my forehead this bright morn, Cyril?" Jonathon asked sardonically. "For, surely you would not attempt such a cork-brained excuse for your behavior under normal circumstances, and goad me, to boot?" He began to travel the confines of the small gazebo and, in the process, inadvertently knocked Cyril's propped leg from its perch.

Cyril straightened. "No need for physicality, Jon. I should say you are the one who should be reprimanded for compromising Miss Lark's position. After all, it was not I who had her visit at such an unholy hour with not hide nor hair of chaperone in sight. What say you to that?"

"I say you are deliberately trying to shift the attention of your indiscretion to other, less important, matters." He looked firmly into his brother's face and shook an adamant finger. "I tell you now, Cyril. You are to stay away from my future wife whenever possible. I do not want her immaculate reputation sullied by your wayward one. Do I make myself clear?" All he needed was Cyril enamored with Lark.

Cyril stood and looked unwaveringly at his older brother. "Clear as glass, Jonathon." The amusement was completely void from him now. "Until this moment I did not realize quite how much you distrusted me. I *am* your brother, after all." Without another word, Cyril turned and stepped from the gazebo.

"Cyril...wait..."

But he didn't, and Jonathon was left to watch his sibling storm towards the manor house. Oh, how he felt like the left shoe devoid of the right. He hadn't intended to roast Cyril quite so much. It was the pressure of it all— First Lark's speech impediment, then Aunt Harriet's by-blow disclosure, the subsequent prolonged absence of Bentley Smythe, and Lark's birthmark—now he had cast out Cyril.

And, as if that were not enough, he had arranged to learn the hand language with which Lark communicated. His first lesson was this very day and he didn't feel quite up to the challenge of having to swallow his ample pride and learn from the likes of an abigail.

Oh, bother! This just would not do.

With determination, he descended the gazebo and made his way back to the house. He would reset Cyril.

Cyril had put on his overcoat and stood diligently buttoning the front when Jonathon at last found him.

"Now, Cyril, don't rush off in apparent dismay. Let's settle this thing before you go. I am quite on mark in saying you have misunderstood me." Jonathon hastened to his brother's side. "It's been a trying fortnight. Let us make amends and be brothers once more." He looked directly into eyes that were a mirror of his own.

"I know I am not a paragon, but I am your brother, Jonathon. And loyal to the end," Cyril said, meeting his brother's gaze.

"And this I know. With all my soul, this I know. I was but upset. I can't speak of all that has materialized these past weeks. I am not myself and I apologize." Jonathon clapped Cyril on the shoulder with a strong grip. "Are we set aright?"

Cyril nodded. A grin spread across his face and his dark eyes brightened. "Yes, brother. We are set aright." He slapped Jonathon on the arm. "Now let me take my leave. I must return home and clean myself up. The ladies await me this eve."

"You call those females with which you gallivant, ladies?" Jonathon teased.

"As close to one as I dare to get. Such a handsome devil as myself, flock among the *ton*? Why, I would be hen-pecked in no time."

They laughed together, and then Jonathon watched his brother get into the ready curricle and urge the horses away.

Jonathon secured the door and turned to look at the staircase. One misunderstanding righted. Now for the difficult measure. Miss Lark Blackwell.

He put one foot toward the stairs and heard a board creek above. He looked up to see Rebekka descending post haste.

"Ah Rebekka, I was about to—"

"Sorry to be late, m'lord," the abigail puffed as she hurried down the stairs. "Miss Lark was in quite a tizzy, she was. I dare not come down at all."

"Yes, I am afraid that was my doing. I was about to speak to her about it."

"Not to worry, m'lord. I tended to her." Rebekka reached the bottom landing and made her way breathlessly to him. "She is a gentle creature more often than not, but I am afraid she inherited her papa's temper. Keeps it hidden quite well most of the time. She is not one to seek other people's wrath, you see. What with being hid away. She don't quite know how to act."

So, Rebekka knew they were hiding. He wondered if she knew why. Certainly, his father's letter had told him the fire had not been an accident, but no clues to intent or perpetrator were included. Perhaps Rebekka knew the answer to these questions. Taking the time to learn the hand language might prove more productive than he first imagined.

He smiled cordially. "No need to make excuses for her, Rebekka. I quite understand her situation."

He directed Rebekka to go into his study while he issued Chauncy to fetch a light meal. The day was still a hatchling, but Jonathon was famished.

When he returned to the room, he found Rebekka seated primly in the same chair Lady Wescotte had occupied while she had dealt him that fateful news.

The memory made his stomach lurch. Soon, Smythe would return and Jonathon would be able to clear up that portion of his father's affairs. Now for the more pressing issue at hand.

Rebekka shifted in the chair and rose when he entered.

He motioned with his hand. "Do sit down. Chauncy will bring in some refreshment shortly." He crossed the room and circled the desk to sit opposite her. "Where shall we begin?" He queried.

She sat and smoothed out her thinning skirts. "Well, m'lord, I thought we would start with the basics, just as when I taught Miss Lark. You see, each letter in the alphabet has a matching hand sign."

"Very well," Jonathon smiled to reassure Rebekka. Although she always seemed to look at him with thoughtful, kind eyes, she appeared a mite apprehensive today.

"Are you quite well, Rebekka? Should we do this another time?"

"I am all right. I find myself a bit nervous, m'lord. After all, Lark was a wee sprite when I taught her the language and not at all the lord of the manor."

"Forget who I am for now, Rebekka. You seem to be a levelheaded abigail, if ever I saw one. I'm quite confident you shall help me understand Miss Lark's words without a dither."

"Thank you, m'lord. You are very kind indeed."

Chauncy entered with a tray of delicate pastries and tea. With a smile to Rebekka and a nod to Lord Somerset, he presently left the room in silence.

"He realizes we are in private conference," Lord Somerset offered at Chauncy's hasty retreat. "Allow me to pour you some tea." He stood and moved to the tray service Chauncy had placed beside the desk.

After quelling the woman's protest that he should not

wait on her, Jonathon prepared Rebekka's tea to her specification, then sat back at his desk and sipped his own. "Let us begin, shall we," he urged.

Rebekka nodded and placed her teacup on the tray. She positioned her fingers. "This is the letter 'A'."

Lord Somerset imitated her. "'A'," he repeated, the pattern-card of students.

Chapter Eleven

The solicitor's outer office was filled with the pungent odor of cheroot as Bentley Smythe said his good-byes to Baron Oscar Reginald. Jonathon waited, somewhat impatiently, for the prolific baron to dispense with the niceties and finally take his leave.

The baron raised his cigar in greeting as he walked past, and Jonathon smiled wordlessly, clutching the papers Lady Wescotte had given him.

When the door closed behind Smythe's other client, the solicitor offered his right hand to Jonathon. "Sorry to keep you waiting, my lord."

Jonathon stood and shook Smythe's hand. "Not to worry," he assured him, sounding much more cordial than he actually felt at the moment. He'd waited a lifetime, it seemed, for the solicitor to return from abroad and was quite impatient to get this mess with Lady Wescotte cleared up in a timely manner.

They walked into the privacy of Smythe's office. "I had several messages from you, Lord Somerset. Is there some problem with your father's will or holdings?"

"Not at all. I wished to see you about this." Lord Somerset handed Mr. Smythe the stack of documents. "My Aunt Harriet came to me with these, and I would like to know the validity of them. They are papers from your office. Is it true that Geoffry Wescotte is truly one of my father's heirs?"

Smythe averted his attention, not once meeting Jonathon's gaze. The solicitor took the papers and laid them on his ample desk without as much as a glance at them. "Please sit down, my lord."

Utter frustration seeped into Jonathon's bones, and dread seized his heart as he looked at the guilt in Bentley Smythe's glassy eyes. He knew at that very instant Aunt Harriet and the papers bespoke the truth.

"See here, Smythe. I am not a sapling any longer. I do not need to sit down. I need the truth and I need it now."

"Please, Lord Somerset, sit down. This is not an easy matter to discuss. For certain, I am not sure I should speak of it at all. It was a confidential matter between your father and me."

Jonathon's blood raged a war within him. "My father is dead, Mr. Smythe. His business is now my own," he bit out.

Smythe looked truly chastised. He expelled a heavy sigh and perched on the corner of his desk. "Very well," he conceded. He nodded everso slightly "Yes. The papers are correct, however, you were never to know."

Jonathon sat down. Aunt Harriet was such a villainous prattlebox; he had wished it to be a mistake, a fabrication she devised to obtain more wealth. But it was true. Hollowness settled in the pit of his stomach. "Tell me the entire story. And do not omit a single detail. If I am to carry on this charade I must know exactly what happened."

Jonathon wondered if he had truly known his father at all. Oh how he prayed his mother had died without knowledge of his father's adultery, for Geoffry's age made it apparent that this deed had been perpetrated before her death. He swallowed the billiard-sized ball in his throat.

"I cannot know the exact circumstances, Lord Somerset. Understand, although I was a friend to your father as well as legal counsel?, I was not privy to the relationship he shared with your mother." Smythe paused, studying his hand as if there were notes for the conversation written on them.

Jonathon watched stone-faced and waited for Smythe to continue. The air between them lay heavy with dread and hesitation, but Jonathon could do nothing to ease the turmoil Smythe was obviously experiencing—his own unrest was much too great for that.

"All...right...then," Smythe faltered. "By the time your father approached me he had already made arrangements with Lady Wescotte. He needed me only for the legality of the settlement, you see."

"There was a child conceived." He stated the obvious with much strain evident in his voice. He slid from the corner of the desk and began to walk the floor beside Jonathon.

With mounting frustration, Jonathon watched the older man's Hessians chew the carpet. "Do sit down, man," Jonathon ground out.

Smythe stopped abruptly, showed an apologetic look, started, stopped, then started again to make his way behind the desk to sit opposite Jonathon.

"Your father, with my aid, drew up an agreement that would ensure no scandal would touch any of his heirs. Lady Wescotte agreed to spend an appropriate time with the late Lady Bertrum. At the time Lady Bertrum was considerably ill as you may recall and so it was not suspected that there was any other reason for Lady Wescotte to visit her sister in the country."

Always overlooking the fact that Aunt Harriet had never done anything so self-sacrificing in all her days. The waspish thought stung Jonathon's mind. And now the old dragon was all but threatening to tell *The Political Register* of Geoffry's true parentage. After raising him from a pup, did she not care about his feelings in the least?

"Are you telling me that not even Lord Wescotte knows of this?" Jonathon asked incredulously.

Smythe nodded. "That is correct. Lady Wescotte was to come back from the country with the newborn after writing Lord Wescotte some time before that she was in the family way and would not travel home until after the event. No one was to learn of it, you see. That is the tragedy of it all."

"I dare not call it a 'tragedy' that I found out the truth, Smythe. After all, it was Aunt Harriet herself who told me. It wasn't some tragic accident that gave up the game."

Smythe shook his balding head quite emphatically. "Oh, was not speaking of yourself, my lord, as much as that of your lady mother."

So the very thing Jonathon dreaded most had happened. His poor mother had known the truth before her death. He dropped his gaze to a spot on the deep red carpet beneath his feet. He hoped the solicitor did not notice the emotion present there. When he had regained his composure, he looked again to Bentley Smythe.

"When did my mother learn of the result of my father's indiscretions?"

"It was the very night she died, my lord."

Jonathon felt as if he had been hit in the head with a lead pipe. He seemed to know his father and mother less and less, as Smythe revealed more and more. It was a dreadful, disjointed feeling of being out of kilter with everything he had ever believed was his life.

"How do you know this?"

"I know because it plagued your father, and after he took in Miss Lark and had no outside connection, I was his only confidant. We were more than business acquaintances, as I mentioned before, and he knew whatever he told me would go no further." Smythe shifted his chair closer to the desk and rested his forearms on the wood.

Jonathon searched his thoughts for answers, for some sort of connection. His mind was a jumbled mess that wanted to be arranged, coupled. The truth about Geoffry, the death of his mother, Lark being sequestered, the fire. He tried to link the incidents together without knowing why, or even if he should. His efforts were in vain. No amount of logic could connect it all.

"Are you positive you would not care for a refreshment?"

"What? Ah," Jonathon shook his head absently, "no thank you."

Smythe stood. "Look, my lord, do not try to think on it too much. It is really nothing of consequence any longer. You now know the truth regarding Geoffry's parentage. By all legalities, you should continue to abide by the contract until the time expires. If you wish me to draft another agreement I shall be happy to do so."

Jonathon looked at Smythe with vacuous eyes. He opened his mouth to speak, then closed it again as nothing profitable came to mind. He raised himself out of the chair and his right arm autonomously offered itself. "Just one more thing, Smythe," he asked hesitantly, "What of Miss Lark, her parentage, the danger to her?"

"I could not begin to elaborate, my lord."

"But I must know." The alarm in his tone echoed throughout the solicitor's chamber and came back at Jonathon; it sounded foreign.

"I'm sorry, my lord. I have no knowledge of either."

Jonathon took his leave without uttering another sound.

****

Jonathon paced the garden. He felt like a pawn in a chess match. He shook his head. The whir of information was too much to comprehend. Who had his father really been, he asked himself one more futile time. It would serve Aunt Harriet right if he dissolved the resolution between her and his father. What would she do? Ruin the reputations of them all? The old dragon just might be that spiteful. She had gone thus far.

Then there was Lark to consider. He was still unsure how she entered into this enlightened information, but he was quite positive there was a connection somewhere. It was too much of a coincidence that his father would ask him to marry and protect the only survivor from the fire in which his mother died—and on the very night she had discovered his indiscretion. Too much of a coincidence indeed. The more he thought about it the more it seemed that Lark might actually be his kinswoman. Yet Jonathon still could not fathom that his father would do such a thing as wed him to his own kin. The very thought churned his stomach. There had to be another explanation.

His feet wandered to and fro while his mind drove in circles. In the end, he decided he would have to know more about the fire, why his father believed it was no accident.

He could hire a Bowstreet Runner, he supposed. They were always trustworthy, efficient detectives. But this matter was much too delicate with which to take chances. He needed help from someone he could trust with his very life—for his very life did depend on it, and Lark's, too, for that matter. Instinct told him she was as much a pawn in this game as he, but then when it came to her, he couldn't rely on his instinct. His fondness of her tended to cloud his judgment.

Only one name came to mind. Drew Hollingsworth. Being in newspapers, he would have the insight, the background information, and he was more trustworthy than a great many members of the *ton*.

Jonathon turned to go back to the house, ready to send Hollingsworth a missive, and saw movement behind the thicket. He walked over to the low-growing bushes and peered over, curious as to who would be out here at this time of the day.

His eyes narrowed when he saw Lark. "Spying on me, Miss Blackwell?" he snapped.

She lowered her head, shaking it emphatically, and he immediate felt remorse.

He was in a foul mood and should not take it out on her. "I am sorry for snapping at you," he said and her head darted up. "Well you don't have to look so surprised," he told her with no amount of delicacy. "I am not so dratted stubborn that I can't apologize when I am in the wrong."

Her brows came together, and her blue eyes studied him in apparent confusion. It did something to his insides to see her thus, to know that he had done her so wrong in days past that now she was taken aback by a simple act of civility. He hadn't intended their relationship to digress so.

He wanted to reach out to her, touch her, reassure her, but he was afraid she would take it as an affront. He had been a veritable ogre.

Instead, he held out a hand. "Look, we have been at each other's throats since the reading of Father's will. Let us make amends, shall we? Then perhaps you will see I'm not the beast you think I am."

"I do not think you are a beast," she signed.

"Slow down, dearest," Jonathon said. Her hands had flown like air through a tube, so quickly he had been able to decipher only one word. Unfortunately, that word had been "beast," and he was not at all sure whether she had said he was a beast or was not.

She looked at him with that confusion in her eyes again. This time it made him smile. She was unaware of his taking instruction in her hand language. "Repeat what you said, only more slowly," he said, explaining no further.

She moved her hands more slowly, deliberately. Her eyes never left him.

"I thought sure you would have labeled me a beast at the very least, perhaps something even more ghastly." He showed her a wry smile.

Lark returned his smile and Jonathon's blood chilled. Did not the shape of her mouth match that of his father's?

****

The square was free of vendors and ominously quiet as Jonathon rounded the corner the next morning. The wheels of his cabriolet mixed with the clopping of Haydn's hooves, becoming a harbinger of things yet unknown. Jonathon's somber mood, already borne in the deadened street, grew even dimmer.

His groom tugged on the reins and Haydn obediently stopped outside the black, wrought iron gate that heralded the house of Drew Hollingsworth.

Jonathon stepped down from the carriage and surveyed the desolate square. Adjusting his tall hat, he tilted his head and peered into the upper storey of Hollingsworth's building, a large white monstrosity that had been handed down when the man's family still owned their title. *That* disgrace had taken place some generations before Hollingsworth came into existence, but it was still a cause for Drew to be looked down upon.

Such was the reason, Jonathon supposed, that Drew had chosen the rather controversial profession of newspapering.

He tugged on the waist of his coat and turned to his groom.

"Collect me on the hour. I shall be no longer than that."

The groom nodded and snapped Haydn's reins. The stallion trotted away, but not before depositing a ghastly smelling present on the pavement behind Jonathon. He looked down, wrinkled his nose, and cast a glance Heavenward as a silent prayer in hopes that this was not a foreshadow of the way his life was to proceed.

With steps that were surer than his mind, he approached the black iron gate, lifted the latch, and went up to the glaring white front door. He was surprised to see Drew himself answer the herald.

"Rexley, old chap, good to see you again. Sorry about your papa." Hollingsworth held out a freckled hand and shook Jonathon's vigorously.

"Where is that Indian fellow you call a butler."

"Sad turn of events, that. Rashid's mother fell ill. I granted him a leave of absence to take care of family business. Hopped a boat to India a fortnight ago." He turned aside. "But enough of that; come in and tell me to what I owe the pleasure of this visit."

Hollingsworth continued to speak as Jonathon entered the ornate vestibule. "If you want tea you will have to make do with improficiency," he joked. "However, I am quite sure I can pour you a brandy without mucking it up too much."

"I am quite fine at present, thank you." Jonathon slipped out of his overcoat and propped it on the coat rack without much care, then gave another healthy tug to the hem of his waistcoat. "I'm in quite a bit of a dilemma. I thought you might be able to help me with a bit of investigation?"

Hollingsworth sliced through his mop of orange hair with thick fingers. "Come into the library," he said and led the way. "You positive about that drink, then?"

"Are you deliberately avoiding the question, Drew, or is something the matter?" Jonathon did not wait for an invitation but rather sat on the gilt-edged, olive green chair.

"Of course I want to help you, it is merely...well...you see...well you would not see, would you, you have harbored yourself away and..."

"Oh, what are you blathering on about, Hollingsworth?" Jonathon's shoelace nerves unraveled further. With growing apprehension, he watched a play of emotions travel his friend's countenance.

Hollingsworth probed Jonathon with worried green eyes. "There has been some gossip of late, Jon. There is word about that you are to take a wife."

Jonathon's mouth opened, but Hollingsworth showed him a quick palm. "No, let me finish. *I*, as you well know, listen not a tot to rumors. But if you are bouncing on the fringes of propriety are you positive it is all the go for the likes of me to aid you in some matter that might better be left to Bow Street?"

Jonathon could feel the rage bubbling inside him like. There were but a handful of people who knew about his betrothal, and they had all sworn their secrecy in light of circumstances.

Someone of the Rexley lineage could not be trusted. And Jonathon had a definite suspicion what name that sneaky culprit bore. She did not know with whom she played. Malice made a home in Jonathon's heart. He hadn't lost a chess match in better than a decade. And he was not about to begin with this most important one.

He crossed one leg over the other and rested a nonchalant arm on the chair rest. "'Tis not a rumor, Drew. That is the precise matter to which I would like to enlist your aid."

Hollingsworth drew thin eyebrows into an even thinner line. "What the devil do you mean 'tis not a rumor. You are in mourning. It wouldn't be proper for you to announce an engagement. And if you recall, old chap, you are a stickler for the rules." Drew came to sit on the edge of the chair next to Lord Somerset.

Under Hollingsworth's severe gaze, Jonathon felt as if he were being interrogated by the King's men. It was quite unnerving, but irritating, all the more. He returned Drew's intensity with a bland gaze.

"You speak the truth," he replied evenly. "I have always felt a responsibility to uphold a certain decorum in light of my father's and brother's weaknesses in that regard. But you know full-well, Drew, that I am not so bound by that stringency that I haven't raised a few eyebrows in the past."

Hollingsworth came to the edge of the chair. "By Jove, I do believe the passing of your father has addled your brain. Have you gone completely mad? This surpasses dancing on the fringes, Jon, this is...well, it is..." he threw his hands up in defeat. "I know not what it is." Hollingsworth shook his head.

"It is not that bad. I am not green enough to attach myself formally to a woman before the oncoming weeks ensue. My wits are fully functional, I assure you. Besides, all the truth be out in the open, it was at the request of my father that I am to marry. I could not very well go against his last wish, could I?" He audibly exhaled, then stood up. "I think I will have a brandy after all." He made his way across the room to the drinks cabinet.

"Do me one up, too," Drew said.

"What a host," Jonathon quipped. As he made his way back to his seat, he inquired one more time. "So, are you willing to come to my aid, or not?"

Hollingsworth took a sip of the brandy Jonathon handed him. "Of course. Anything for you. I daresay you are the only friend of merit I have. But what do you want me to do?"

"This is all in the strictest of confidences, Drew. If anyone were to discover the truth of things, I can scarce imagine what might happen. This is exactly why I cannot trust even a Bow Street runner. One never knows what another will do for a price, and the price of discovery is too great to risk."

Jonathon took pause as the dreadful thought of harm befalling Lark popped into his head. Odd, how she had wormed her way into his being so strongly that the thought of losing her caused his heart to twist. More than her deficiency, his primary fear now was the skulking possibility that he might discover something much more detrimental.

That nagging thought mercilessly held him prisoner. He exorcised it as best he could and proceeded to fill in Hollingsworth about the fire, Lark, and his father's actions. "The truth will set you free," he had been taught in church as a child. And regardless of how fearful that truth might be, he had to know what it was.

Chapter Twelve

Jonathon sat under the large shade tree studying the notes he had taken during his last session with Rebekka. It was more difficult than he'd expected to think in English and sign in French, but he was glad to be able to understand Lark first-hand.

He had not seen her since the garden two days ago, yet he would dine with her this eve and wanted to apologize for the abrupt manner in which he had left. He had just been so startled by the resemblance she had shown to his father.

He shook his head and tried to concentrate on speaking with his hands. He leaned his head back on the tree trunk and closed his eyes.

"*What sadness lengthens Romeo's hours?*"

Jonathon opened his eyes at Cyril's Shakespearean recital. "Are you here to irritate me, or is there some useful reason for your presence?"

"Tut, tut, Jonathon. You have longer claws than that of Aunt Harriet. I would take a scissors to them if I were you. It is most unbecoming of a gentleman."

Jonathon conceded, knowing his outburst was born more of an irritation with his own situation than with Cyril.

He attempted to apologize by following Cyril's lead and quoting the next line from Romeo and Juliet. "*Not having that which, having makes them short.*"

Cyril did not continue the charade, but rather, to Jonathon's aggravation, took up with reality. "Out of sorts with our lovely Miss Lark, are we?"

"She is not 'our lovely Miss Lark'. I thought *we* cleared that up. She is *my* Miss Lark."

"Can't say as I remember you being this protective of something since Papa brought home that foal when you were nine and I wanted to ride him."

85

"Well, he was mine, and you were but five years old. You would have killed yourself and injured the foal."

"I see you have a keen ability to shift the subject. An asset, I assure you, but one that does not work so easily on me. I know you too well, brother. Besides, I saw you wiggling your fingers and waving your hands about. Even I do not think you would go to such lengths if you did not care for the miss."

"I have no choice. I wouldn't be able to live with the guilt were I to let all pass to you."

Cyril clutched his heart dramatically. "You wound me."

To Jonathon's relief, his brother seemed not to notice the *faux pas* of his statement. He had to be careful not to let anyone know he was being forced by decree to take Lark to wife. He was certainly growing weary of being in constant mind of the secrecy.

Jonathon sighed. "You know I don't mean to sound so harsh. I merely state the obvious truth. You are neither ready, nor willing to settle in to such responsibilities. It is an observation, not a criticism."

Cyril chuckled. "I know," he said. "And you have the right of it. I wouldn't wish to be you for anything in the world. Save, Miss Lark, that is." He smiled as Jonathon clenched his jaw. "Well, I must be honest with you, Jon. You are, after all, my brother. I would not for the world burrow in on your claim. I do have some manners. But mark my words. Do not ever bring her to tears." He offered a hand to Jonathon. "Do get up and we shall have a drink."

Jonathon ignored his brother's hand and rose from the grass of his own accord. "You will not let it be known, that I must study so intently to learn this language of hers?"

Cyril clapped Jonathon on the back then threw his arm around Jonathon's shoulder. "Your secret is safe with me. It would not be all the pretty if she were to find out you have more than a stone for a heart, eh?"

Jonathon eyed his brother seriously. Perhaps Cyril was not such a wastrel after all.

They walked to the house in companionable silence.

"So tell me, what had you looking all vexed out

there?" Cyril asked as Jonathon poured them a healthy portion of brandy.

Jonathon rounded the drinks cabinet and handed a glass to his brother. "Nothing serious. I am just befuddled by Miss Lark."

"Well, there you have it," Cyril surmised, suddenly wise.

Jonathon pivoted to look at his brother. "There you have what?"

Cyril sipped his drink thoughtfully. "'It', Jonathon. The problem at hand."

Jonathon let out a disgusted groan. "I have no idea what you are on about."

"I wonder, have you ever noticed a resemblance to your Miss Lark Blackburn and the late child we once knew, Lark Blackwell of the house of that name?"

Jonathon froze, his body as rigid as the barrel of a pistol. He was at a loss for words for several moments before he actually could utter hoarsely, "You see some resemblance?"

Cyril nodded calmly. "Quite. I find it extraordinary. Almost as if a ghost has come back from the dead. Frightfully eerie if I dwell on it." He shuddered.

"I cannot say I had thought of the like."

"Mmm," Cyril muttered. "And I suppose it has not crossed your mind another connection to that fateful eve? That it was hence that Father booted us out. Quite strange, that. Can't say as it had crossed my mind until just recently. The connection, that is. And now suddenly there is another fair Lark in our midst—with almost an identical name. Do you find it most strange?"

"I suppose if I had a suspicious and inventive mind I might find it intriguing. But strange? I think not. Just coincidence." Jonathon looked at his brother in earnest. "People, Cyril, do not come back from the dead."

"Yes, I suppose you are right. But, tell me, have you had any contact with that dratted Somerset Ghost the gossipmongers run rampant with?"

"I do not pay heed to gossipmongers. And of course, I have not had contact with any such Somerset Ghost. One does not exist. Have you gone completely daft, Cyril?"

"No. Not completely." Cyril downed the rest of his

brandy.

The brothers studied one another in silence.

Jonathon straightened his back a little under Cyril's scrutiny. The man had an expression of regality on his features that was quite vexing. It had the effect of making Jonathon feel very much the cat's paw.

But there was something much more important that he discovered as he studied his brother—He was quick-witted to a fault. In normal circumstances, this would have troubled Jonathon, but instead it gave him measure to know that Cyril could be trusted with a secret. For, if Cyril suspected a connection between the mysterious Miss Lark and the Lark of the Blackwell family, he had done well to keep it under his hat.

"I am quite beginning to see you in a new light," Jonathon said, taking his glass and setting it on the table.

"I can't be sure if you mean that as a compliment or a jibe, but I am willing to give you the benefit of the doubt." Cyril made his glass a companion of Jonathon's. "I must be off. I shall see you on the morrow." He started towards the door.

"What is tomorrow?" Jonathon inquired.

Cyril turned and blessed his brother with a mischievous grin. "Why, tomorrow is not today and bound to be full of adventures yet experienced."

"Egads! Give me strength," Jonathon mumbled as he watched his brother depart.

****

"You should have been there, my lord, it was wonderful!"

Jonathon delighted in the animation of Lark's entire body as she told him of her outing. Since he revealed he was learning her hand language, she had become a veritable chatterbox. Her hands moved with such quickness that he could scarcely comprehend all the words, but her enthusiasm invigorated him. He sipped on his after-dinner sherry and watched the candlelight play across her face and hands.

"I must admit I quite acted the child at first, poking my head out of the carriage window to allow the crisp morning air to wash my face. Oh, the streets were still wet with dew and the shop fronts, oh, the shops!" Lark stilled her hands and looked at him rather sheepishly. "I am sorry. I have talked and talked this eve without a thought to boring you, my lord."

"No, no, do go on, my dear. I am interested in your first experience off the estate."

Lark graced him with the widest of grins. "Carriages teemed the streets, and the clatter of horses' hooves was like an orchestra of music. Ladies and footmen covered the lanes. Bond Street is the most enticing place. I can scarce describe it."

"I am very happy to hear your experience was quite pleasant."

Her smile faded. "It was not all pleasant, my lord. There was a time when I was quite terrified."

He leaned forward and touched her gloved arm. She suddenly resembled a hapless child. "What should terrify you about Bond Street?"

"The ladies in the mantuamaker's. It was harrowing to the complete to have to use my hands to speak. I thought the lot of them would fall away from the counter like dominos."

He laughed, and she looked as if he had stuck her with a dagger. "I am sorry. I did not mean to find pleasure in your formidable experience. It was merely the image of the ladies falling down." He held out a hand to her. "Come. Let's retire to the library and you may finish your most intriguing story."

She allowed him to help her stand then eased her hand out of his grip. "And I saw your lovely cousin, Marie. We partook of nuncheon and dessert at a delightful place called Gunter's. The ices were impeccable."

As they made their way from the dining room to the library, Jonathon tugged the bell-pull. Chauncy appeared in the great room. "We shall take tea in the library,"

"Yes, m'lord."

Jonathon turned his eyes back to Lark. "So you like Marie, I gather?"

Lark stopped walking and turned to him, her hands flying in that same animated fashion. "Oh, yes. She is a dear, not at all like Lady Wescotte. It is hard to believe they share relations." She clapped her hand over her mouth. "I am sorry," she quickly signed. "I completely forgot myself. I hope I do not embarrass you thus in view of the *ton*. That just would not do." She looked up directly into his face. "I am sorry," she signed, her fingers and body slowly deflated from that effervescence she had previously shown.

He found her charming beyond compare. Without thought, he took her hand in his and gently brushed his lips against her gloved palm. "You are like buttercups and honey, my dearest," he said.

She gazed up at him with a caressing glow in her eyes. For a moment, he thought she might speak, but then she lifted herself onto her toes and kissed him lightly on the cheek.

Her mouth was soft and warm. He had never experienced so gentle an embrace, and it touched him to the core. He tightened his grip around her fingers and pulled her closer, then raised his other hand to stroke her soft cheek. Her cornflower blue eyes fluttered closed; she looked like an angel.

He closed his eyes and inhaled the lavender scent of her. How could he have ever thought someone so innocent could be deceitful?

He took her lips with his own, and she leaned into him. He could feel her dainty curves pressing against his body and felt an urgency well within him. He released her hand he held between them and pulled her ever closer.

She framed his face with her hands in an embrace that sent spirals of need through his body. She pulled his head closer to hers and moaned against his lips. And suddenly it was as if someone had drenched him with a bucket of cold water.

He shoved her away from him with such force he had to reach out again to keep her from tipping over. He dropped her hand and stepped backwards himself. "What the devil am I doing? I have birds in the attic!" He noticed her startled, hurt expression. "Do not look at me thus. We may have to wed, but we will certainly never, ever...ever," he repeated finally, at a loss for an appropriate word. He raked his hand through his hair. "Bloody Hell!" The oath escaped him before he could pull it back. He bolted past Lark and above stairs to his chamber. What kind of man was he to make love to a woman who might very well be his relative?

Chapter Thirteen

Oft-times in the midst of turmoil genius sprouts, Lord Somerset thought as he made his way through West London. So many quandaries had plagued his mind of late, that he had scarce been able to solve any of them. Then, last evening, a brilliant idea popped into his head for dealing with Aunt Harriet. With a little luck and crafty persuasion, he would teach the toplofty old squab a lesson she would be hard-pressed to forget.

Lord Somerset greeted the house steward with a warm smile. "Good morrow Simpson. Do announce my arrival to Lady Wescotte."

"How do you do, Lord Somerset. Allow me to extend my condolences," Simpson said, stepping back to allow Lord Somerset entrance.

Jonathon pulled off his riding gloves and handed them to the steward. "I trust Lady Wescotte is up and about?"

"Yes, my lord, however, you do come unannounced." Simpson looked a little perturbed, but Jonathon ignored it. Arriving unannounced was part of the plan, part of the pleasure. Aunt Harriet despised impropriety—especially in one of her kin. It would definitely set her in a tither, and he would, no doubt, have the upper hand.

"Do not fear for your position," Lord Somerset said, shrugging out of his overcoat and handing it to the servant. "I shall be sure to tell Lady Wescotte the fault was all mine."

The steward seemed truly dumbfounded by Lord Somerset's outright gall, and Jonathon couldn't remember feeling so completely full of mischief in ages. It felt good, and made him wonder if Cyril's waywardness had rubbed off on him in some fashion.

"If you do not mind waiting, I will announce you, my lord."

Jonathon nodded and watched the butler waddle away.

When next Simpson appeared, he looked quite bedraggled and Jonathon had the decency to feel sorry for him. The steward bowed politely. "Lady Wescotte will see you now," he said on a sigh. "However, I am to inform you it is the only exception she will make."

"That so? Well I suppose we'll see."

"Yes, my lord," Simpson replied, his tone echoing his doubt of Jonathon's ability to overturn the lady's decision.

Jonathon found his aunt in the parlor with a cart of tea next to her ample chair. She waved a ringed finger at Simpson. "Leave us," she demanded. "And do not disturb us unless someone is dying. And then only if it is someone of importance," she called after the departing butler. "I suppose you want tea now that you have interrupted my solitude. For heaven's sake, Jonathon, it is only half past eleven. An ungodly hour to take visitors."

He came into the room and stood directly in front of her. She looked unusually over-weight this morning, he thought. Pink was definitely not her color. The bombazine morning dress distended around her in the chair, making her look quite like one of those new-fangled hot air balloons.

Jonathon smiled. "Not mourning, Aunt Harriet?" He asked pointedly.

She glanced down at the rose-colored fabric she wore. "I am alone in my home, Jonathon. And not expecting callers, I might add."

"Are you not going to offer me a chair?"

She waved an impatient hand in his direction. "As you please. For what are you here? You have spoken with Mr. Smythe, I doubt it not?"

Jonathon sat perched on the end of a chair opposite that of his aunt. "I have."

"And?" Lady Wescotte huffed in obvious disgust at the length of time her nephew insisted on detaining her. She dwarfed her teacup in her chubby hands. "Do you take tea?" The question was intoned with irritated cordiality.

"No thank you. I don't wish to be a nuisance."

"If you wished that, you shouldn't have arrived

unannounced," she shot back.

"Yes, well, I am here and ready to discuss business."

"Well do get on with it then."

"Smythe admitted the truth regarding the parentage of Geoffry," Jonathon said evenly. He slid back in the seat and watched the look of triumph envelop Lady Wescotte's face. She didn't speak for several seconds. It was as if she wallowed in victory while awaiting Jonathon to continue.

When he did not, she replaced her teacup on the teacart and leaned forward. "So? Am I to assume you will now continue the endowment due me until the contract's end?"

"Aunt Harriet, you know I am a man of honor. I wouldn't dream of trying to cheat you out of what you rightly deserve."

"Good," she snapped, almost too quickly. She smiled then. "What I meant to say, Jonathon, is that I had every faith you would do what is right."

"Oh, I know exactly what you meant, Aunt Harriet."

She frowned at him for a moment before pasting a satisfied smile to her face once again. "The allowance for this month is, of course, past due. Am I to assume you will distribute that portion immediately and then proceed on course as the agreement states?" She picked up her teacup and tipped it to her lips.

"No."

Tea sputtered from Lady Wescotte's mouth in the most unbecoming fashion, and it took all of Jonathon's concentration not to laugh at his overset aunt. Phase one of his plan was much more successful than he could have imagined. He only hoped she would respond just as aptly when he completed this portion and implemented the final stage.

"What do you mean, 'no'?"

"I mean you would be mistaken to assume such things. I will not appropriate the belated portion immediately, nor will I forward any more portions to you."

He paused for effect and watched all color drain from the woman's face. Her florid cheeks turned a pasty-yellowed hue, and her lips deepened to purple. A slight twinge of compassion made him continue promptly to put her out of her misery.

"I do not feel my father lived up to his responsibility adequately, Aunt Harriet. I vow to do much better by you and Geoffry…"

Her face lit up like a dark London alley suddenly drenched in sunlight.

"…You should never have been burdened with the raising of a son not your own. I propose to take the boy off your hands and continue with the raising of him personally."

The light in her face extinguished. Her lips flapped soundlessly and the teacup rattled in the saucer. She promptly put the china on the serving cart. "Am I to take it that you think I have been an inadequate guardian to Geoffry?" She asked when she once again found her tongue.

Lord Somerset shook his head adamantly. "Not at all, dear lady. I admire your selfless sacrifice in shouldering my father's responsibility. In fact, I thought to reward you for your commendable efforts," Lord Somerset said evenly. "I shall have Smythe draw up a new agreement. I shall deliver to you a lump sum as payment for your past trouble, and I shall take Geoffry off your hands. Is that acceptable to you, Aunt Harriet?"

"We—we—well, I suppose…are you quite positive…I mean do you…What do you know about raising a young boy?"

"As I was one myself once, I daresay a good deal more than you."

"Well, I never. The impertinence." She struggled to her feet and stared down at him with fierce eyes. "You think you know. Well, we'll see. Take him. Take him. And we'll see who knows about the upbringing of children." She showed him her back. "Good day," she said, then left the room.

Jonathon sat for a good deal of time with a curve on his lips he was unable to straighten. He couldn't have staged a better response had he been a puppeteer and Aunt Harriet the puppet.

He rose from the chair, smoothed his tails, and readied to make his leave. If he were going to pull this off without discord, he would have to have Smythe draw up some papers.

****

Lark winced, a mirror of the pain etched on Jonathon's features. She backed away from him. "I am so sorry. I just cannot seem to get the hang of this quadrille," she signed slowly.

"'Tis quite all right, my dear. It would probably do you all the better were there more than just the two of us here. It is awfully difficult to get the right idea without the benefit of all the proper partners and music."

"But your poor mashed toe," she signed.

"Shall we go back to something slower once again? The waltz perhaps?" He suggested with a distinct air of hopefulness in his tone.

"Are you quite sure that would be all right? After all, I would be all the more closer to your poor feet, my lord."

"Ah, yes, but then, I would also have a firmer grip on your movements, would I not?"

The heat rose up Lark's neck. Trying to ignore her embarrassment, she silently picked up the hem of her peach gown. She so wished she could control her feelings. She was sure they betrayed her, for Jonathon eyed her in a most uncomfortable manner, his dark eyes seemingly piercing her thoughts as an expert marksman finds a bulls-eye.

She averted her gaze and held out her bent arm as she had been instructed. She felt him near as he stepped up to take her hand. Her fingers tingled in anticipation even before she felt his flesh touch her gloved hand. When his warmth kissed her palm, her knees liquefied.

She stared blankly at his cravat, counting silently as he whirled her around the empty library.

"That's it, my dear," he coaxed her gently. "I am quite positive when we announce our engagement I will be the envy of all."

Her gaze darted to him, then. Could he have meant that? She wished desperately to ask him, to hear the affirmation of his words, but he was holding her hand, and so she could not converse. Her mouth came open, but she closed it again. That was a useless decoration on her face.

He abruptly stopped waltzing and studied Lark with a scrutiny that made her breath catch. Silence stretched between them but she experienced no awkwardness. If anything, she relished the fact that he had not yet let her go. Her eyes locked with his in a hypnotic charge that sizzled through her entire body. Breathing was a labor.

"You are very beautiful, Miss Lark."

Suddenly her lungs filled with air.

"But I am quite certain you already knew this."

She shook her head slowly and attempted to ease her hand from his grasp. She wanted to deny his words. He shouldn't think he was going to be joined to a simpering, conceited woman who needed false flattery.

Jonathon tightened his grip on her hand so she could not free it to speak. She pulled once again—although, she admitted not putting much strength into her effort. Still he did not let go.

He smiled down at her.

"I will allow no one to ridicule your handicap, and I will allow no one to sully your reputation. You have my word as a gentleman on that," he said.

He cocked his head to one side and studied her from a different angle as if she were a rare piece of art.

"You are like a delicate butterfly..."

An odd quiver in the softness of his voice captivated Lark.

"...hidden away in a cocoon only to be revealed at God's own choosing. Beautiful and unique yet innocent and dainty..." he paused, and she waited, intent on his mouth, the anticipation of his words almost unbearable. "easily captured in a man's net," he concluded.

She swallowed the lump of emotion that snagged in her throat. He sounded so melancholy, yet so arduous, as if he truly ached for her well-being. It caused her to want to speak to him, to tell him verbally all the tumultuous yearnings and doubts inside her.

But she could not. A chasm yawned inside her. She would never be good enough for him. Tears pricked her eyes, and she quickly studied the floor at her side. With a brute force borne of desperation, she wrenched free of his grasp and fled the room.

Jonathon felt the warmth drain from his hand as he watched Lark run from the room. His gaze fell mechanically to his empty, cold hand. He was alone. Had not felt so alone, in fact, since the day he had been forced out of this very house by his father.

And he did not know what to do about it.

****

It had been three days since Lark had abandoned him and their dance lesson, and now, as they were finally sharing another meal, he'd bungled what he wanted to say one more time—only this time, it was his hands that refused to work correctly rather than his mouth. Lark reached across the dining table and covered his hands with her own. Instantly he froze, his eyes transfixed on the creamy, soft hand that encased his own. She was warm. As she absently began to rub the pad of her thumb against the back of his hand, tiny shivers of awareness skittered down his chest and into his loins. He thought he would lose his sanity. He closed his eyes and willed his unfettered emotion into restraint.

It was an innocent, comforting movement on her part. She had no idea of the havoc her caress played on his senses, but he feared that if she did not stop, indeed all sense would be banished from him.

As if in tune with his very thought, her thumb stilled. His eyelids flew open, and their gazes locked as he searched her face for something as unknown as it was needed.

The sconce light flicked across her face, illuminating her blue eyes. They glimmered like the light, soft and inviting, and the urge to draw her face to his, virtually undid him. He wanted to feel her soft, untouched lips on his, caress the softness of her face.

But he did not.

He quickly snatched his gaze and his hand away from her.

"I am but lousy at this," he grated, refusing to look into her face. "How ever am I to make people believe we have been secretly in love for ages if I do not understand your language fluently before the announcement of our engagement?" He drew in a heavy breath and expelled it with a force borne of frustration.

He got up and moved around the room. When his eyes settled on her once again, she appeared out of sorts, melancholy and distant.

"You look quite pale, my dear. Are you all right?"

She nodded slowly, disjointedly, as if it pained her to move her head. His emotions ran amok, like a piece of torn paper in a whirlwind. "What is the matter," He said softly.

She shook her head. "Nothing," she signed.

He took a step towards her.

She showed him her palm, and he froze. "It's nothing," she signed with angry fingers.

Frustration pound Jonathon's chest. "Miss Lark, heavens. Do speak your mind. You have me quite at sea. First sitting there all prim and lovely, the next eyeing me as if I had two heads attached at the neck."

Of a sudden, the sadness in her eyes transformed to something harder.

Her hands flew rapidly, her entire upper body flinging about. "Well that is just it, is it not? I cannot speak my mind!"

Jonathon, startled by her abrupt outburst, had been unable to decipher anything she said, but it was quite obvious in her quick, substantial movements that she was extremely overset. He was a little undone, himself. To be true, he was botching the sign language, but he was trying. Did she not understand that? Her hands were in a frenzy that seemed would never end.

"Please calm yourself, child. I daresay I cannot understand what you say when you move so suddenly."

A stone had leadened Lark's heart as she realized the truth in heartless clarity. He did not want to learn sign language for her sake, but for that of appearance. That was the only reason he was trying so hard. She was a fool to have ever hoped he would care for her. She had spent the last three days lamenting over her own deficiencies, over the realization that she would never be good enough for him. She had known the truth then, but no matter how much she reminded herself of reality of her situation, hope refused to die. She ached for him to love her.

She cast her eyes to his and found him raptly watching her. The heat crept up her neck, and settled as a huge lump in her throat. She would never be anything to him but a deficient child whom he were being forced to marry. What a farce her life had become. Slowly she signed, "I must go."

She started to rise, but he grabbed her wrist. "No," he said evenly. Mutely they studied one another without moving, she bent over the table with her bottom only inches off the chair and he, holding her wrist without sign of ever letting go.

She felt the familiar sting of tears behind her eyes and willed all her strength to evaporate them before they spilled.

"Is this a battle of the wills or something substantial with which I should concern myself?"

His flat, emotionless words cut like a broadsword through butter. Lark slowly lowered herself back into the chair, and he released her wrist. Spent and tired, she wished only to escape him for a while.

"That's better," he said. "Now what brought on that outburst? Praytell, for it is above me."

"I am sorry, my lord," Lark told him with her hands. "Forgive me."

"Your answer circumvents the question."

"It is the only answer I can provide at the moment," Lark told him, sure to keep her movements slow and pronounced.

"Can or will, I wonder."

She lowered her gaze to the empty plate in front of her. "Dinner was lovely, my lord. Thank you for a wonderful meal, but I am tired and wish to take my leave."

"What about me frightens you, Miss Lark? Is it merely a case of doubting my ability to care for you in the manner my father did?"

She did not answer, completely perplexed by his query.

"For I assure you, I hold my responsibilities in high regard. I have mentioned before, I will not allow harm to befall you, nor will you lack for any need that may arise during our marriage."

"I am of a mind that you will fulfill your responsibility in the most honorable manner, my lord," Lark signed, wishing this interlude were at an end. "Don't concern yourself over me. I have never doubted your abilities or intentions."

He showed her a forced smile. "If you truly tire, I won't keep you any longer." He rose and came to stand behind her chair.

Lark watched him until he was out of her vision, and when she felt his gentle tug on the back of the chair, lifted herself out of the seat. Slowly, she turned to face him.

She had been dismissed, of that she had no doubt, but there was something odd in his eyes that left her wondering if he bore anger towards her, or mere indifference.

Bowing her head slightly, she thanked him in sign for a lovely meal and turned to leave.

"Lark." His voice stopped her. He made almost no sound as he placed a hand on her arm and turned her to face him. She looked up into his face, and his eyes conveyed unrest. Lark's heart tore. Would it always be this difficult?

"Lark," he said again. He squeezed her arm ever so slightly, then leaned down and pressed his lips to her forehead. She closed her eyes, an explosion of conflicting emotions tearing at her. "I'm sorry," he said against her skin. He pulled away and looked into her eyes. "Please try to understand, I am doing my utmost to care for you. I know this is difficult for you. It is difficult for me as well." His gaze dropped to the carpet. "More difficult than you can imagine."

Lark's heart met his gaze on the floor at their feet, and she left it there as she turned and fled to the sanctuary of her chambers, his words echoing in her head: *More difficult than you can imagine.*

Chapter Fourteen

"I've pressed your ivory jaconet," Rebekka told Lark.

Lark stood staring out the window. In the distance, she could barely see the church steeple kissing the sky. The fog was still thick. "It looks dreadfully cold outside," she signed, turning to face her abigail.

"That is no reason to wear a long face," Rebekka replied. "Come and let's get you ready for the day."

Silently, Lark crossed the room and allowed Rebekka to remove her dressing gown and slip the slender jaconet gown onto her body.

"When do you suppose it should be appropriate to don the new gowns?" Lark glanced at the wardrobe in the corner, remembering the lovely outing she had enjoyed while ordering the gowns that Penelope had fetched for her when they were ready. She had been tempted to wear one of them at supper last evening, but once the evening had soured, she was glad Rebekka saw fit to talk her out of it.

"As I said last night. When you make your first appearance in society, you will want to look all new. That's the way it's done."

"Yes, but no one will see if I am to wear the gowns beforehand." Perhaps if she were to put on one of the new baroque gowns today, her gray mood would lighten. As it was, her mood was as dark as the clouds out of doors.

Rebekka stepped back and viewed her charge with quiet wisdom. "Lord Somerset would see, my dear, and you want to surprise him as much as any. More so, if you truly wish to capture his heart."

"Why do you suppose Lord Peter told us such a story about Jona—Lord Somerset caring for me? Surely he must have known it would be discovered."

Rebekka shuffled Lark over to the dressing table and sat her down in front of the looking glass. "Perhaps it was not a lie, miss, perhaps it was the truth."

Lark scoffed, but did not say a word with her hands. Rebekka didn't understand. She hadn't been present when Jonathon had said he was only learning sign language for appearance's sake, or when he had pushed her away with obvious disdain, or when he had...Lark halted her musings. There was no need to dwell on things. She must be realistic. She had two choices. Marry Jonathon and spend a life in his presence tormented by the fact that he had married her out of obligation only, or leave Somerset Manor and spend a life not in his presence, tormented by the fact that he would have married her out of obligation only.

Lark scowled at her reflection. Rebekka had brushed Lark's hair in short order, arranging the fine, shimmering locks and pinning them skillfully on one side of her face. Tiny golden tendrils curled naturally all around her face creating an artful frame. It did not seem to matter the skill or time Rebekka put forth, Lark was still plain.

She thought of Marie Beauchamps. How pretty Jonathon's cousin was, a touch of rouge and a hint of lip color to enhance her simple beauty. Lark had no such luxuries to enhance her appearance

Her eyes moved to Rebekka's reflection. "Do you think we could add some things to my toilette before I am to come out to the *ton*?"

"Be still a minute," Rebekka requested kindly. "I have but a few more pins to keep your hair in place."

Lark stilled her hands and waited while Rebekka put the finishing touches on her hair.

Still, it didn't do any good. She was plain as the day was long.

"I should say we could add whatever pleases God," Rebekka said. "Your Lord Somerset has seen fit to give you a tidy allowance."

Lark was thoughtful for a moment. "He does take his responsibility of me to heart, does he not?"

Rebekka widened a grin. "I suppose that's not all he has taken to heart."

"You are much too much a romantic," she signed, a wistful smile on her face.

Her smile faded at a knock on the door.

"I thought you said Lord Somerset left word he would be in London for the day's majority?" Lark signed.

"I did, my lady. To be sure it is probably Penelope or Chauncy come to see if you are ready to breakfast." Rebekka moved to the door and opened it with a smile that faded the very moment the portal was fully undone.

Apprehension seized Lark. She banged a hand on the dressing table to get Rebekka's attention but the abigail had become a statue. All manner of ghastly possibilities ran through Lark's head—the most disturbing: what if some injury had come to Jonathon? Her heart constricted. No. She refused to consider that.

Hesitantly she rose from the ornately padded bench, her slippered feet carrying her silently to stand at the threshold of the door. Her intake of breath was audible in the heavy hush of the darkened, empty morning. Relief and anxiety mingled in her throat. Her eyes darted from Cyril to Rebekka and back several times more before Cyril broke the awkward silence.

"I did not mean to startle you, Miss Lark."

Water stained his overcoat in round droplets that darkened the woolen fabric. His hair was frost dampened and curling at the ends. The reticent look in his eye made him seem like a contrite little boy. She could not help but be amused by his presence at her door. Her mood relaxed a little.

"Tell him it is most inappropriate for a gentleman to meet a lady in her chambers," she signed to Rebekka.

When Rebekka did not answer, but remained as stiff as an icicle on a winter's day, Lark nudged her none too gently.

The abigail clutched the spot on her arm where Lark's elbow had connected hard. "Wh-what, my lady?" Rebekka stammered.

Lark repeated her request with much patience and Rebekka obediently turned to Cyril and interpreted Lark's statement.

A smile drew across Cyril's lips and he regained that knavish countenance Lark already knew was uniquely Cyril's. His eyes fell on her, twinkling and utterly puckish. "My lovely Miss Lark, do you not realize it is ever so much more inappropriate for a young lady such as yourself to dwell in the same house with a gentleman outside the benefit of matrimony. And completely *alone!* Heavens! What were the world to discover it?" He drew a dramatic hand to his cheek and looked all the shocked.

"Tell him he is strictly incorrigible," Lark instructed Rebekka.

Rebekka's eyes widened. "I will do no such thing," she gasped. "What bad manners that would be."

"As if it is not bad manners for my abigail to reprimand me in front of my future brother-in-law?" Lark countered, not particularly perturbed by Rebekka's words.

"If I do not correct your waywardness now, what will you do in but a short time when mourning is finished?"

"I should fare much better if people think I have a firm hand with my servants!" Lark signed rapidly.

"Of all the—"

"Do you suppose I could participate in this conversation," Cyril cut in.

The women's heads swiveled towards him, and he smiled widely at them. "It is a little discomfiting to hear but one half of a conversation," he told them. "Besides, I really must get out of this wet coat and near a warm fire before I catch my death." He craned his neck between the two women and eyed the dying fire across the room. "Looks as if you could do with a strapping man to stoke the fire up a tad."

A disgruntled sound escaped Rebekka's lips, but she had the sense and manners to add not anything verbal to it.

Lark sighed and drew her gaze away from the fire and back to Cyril. "Allow him entry," she signed to Rebekka.

"Do come in," she said resignedly to Cyril.

"This is not quite the thing, is it, Mr. Rexley?" Lark ventured.

"Do you still have your writing tablet?"

Lark nodded slowly wondering why she should need her tablet.

"Do let us converse in private. I have much to discuss," Cyril told her.

Rebekka stepped forward before Lark even had the chance to speak. "I must strongly object, Master Cyril. It is highly wayward for the young miss to be alone with a gentleman."

Cyril chuckled at Rebekka's verve. "I must say, Miss Lark, you certainly have an avid abigail. Why, it would almost seem as if I had asked you to—well, never mind," he stopped himself. "I must remember my tongue. May I get comfortable?" He turned to Rebekka. "Is it all right with you, dear dragon, if I remove my coat and add a log or two to the fire?"

"You lack manners," Rebekka said, unrepentant.

Cyril laughed outright and gave Lark a look full of mirth. "She says that as if it is a revelation from God." He unbuttoned his overcoat and shrugged out of it.

"Should I ask you to hang it, or would you prefer to hang me instead." He held out the coat for Rebekka to take.

She grunted. "Like night and day," she muttered, taking the coat and finding a place for it.

"Very well," Cyril said to Lark. "Keep your chaperon to translate for us." Then he moved closer and leaned into her ear. "She is a trustworthy dragon is not she?"

"Miss Lark, I must insist you instruct him not to refer to me by such offensive names."

Lark nodded, not knowing what to think of the turn of events of the morning. "Do not call Rebekka offensive names," she signed.

Rebekka dropped her head in an exaggerated "I told you so" nod. "There. I am no dragon, sir," she said to Cyril haughtily.

"My deepest apology," he said, although it was obvious to Lark he was far from remorseful.

He added two healthy sized logs to the fire and extended a hand to the chair opposite him in an offering for Lark to be seated.

Nervously, she looked to Rebekka before taking a seat.

Cyril sat opposite her, tilting his body toward the fire and vigorously buffing his hands together. "So," he said, looking into the fire. "How came you to live here? This could not have been my brother's doing. He is much too proper for such a thing." He glanced her way.

"You will not reveal it, Mister Rexley?" Lark asked

cautiously through Rebekka's interpretation.

Cyril shrugged. "Why should I?"

His answer was not as comforting to Lark as she had hoped. But she could not think that he would wish to disgrace his own brother.

"How came you to live here?" he asked again.

This time it was Lark's turn to raise her shoulders. Rebekka, standing between them like a barrage of guard dogs, translated her answer. "Lord Peter brought me."

Cyril opened his mouth but it was not his voice that next met Lark's ears.

Chapter Fifteen

"What is the meaning of this?" Lord Somerset's words split the air like a cleaver. All eyes spun to meet his awesome frame in the open doorway. His face was ruddy from cold and emotion, his closed fists held immovable.

Cyril stood. "There you are. Come in. Join us," he said to his brother, seemingly not the least bit disturbed at being discovered in Lark's chambers.

A muscle worked in Jonathon's jaw. "I repeat," he ground out through clenched teeth, "what is the meaning of this?"

Cyril waved him away with an impatient hand. "For goodness' sake, Jon, calm yourself, and come in. It's no shame to have your secret found out by me. I am not one to blather it to the whole of society."

"How did you get into the house?" Jonathon closed the distance between them, and Rebekka jumped out of the way, to keep from being trampled beneath Jonathon's heedless steps.

Cyril cocked his head to one side. "Well," he drawled. "I came in through the kitchen."

"And Penelope? Chauncy? Did they allow you admittance? I shall dismiss them both."

"Oh, do not be so pompous! Of course, they did not allow me admittance. This is my childhood home, and I daresay I have as much right to be here as do you, brother."

Jonathon heaved in a breath and turned to Lark. After their barely-amicable meal of last evening, he did not want to force his wrath on her. He calmed his tone considerably. "Did you not think it unwise for Cyril to be within your chambers?"

She signed her reply slowly.

"No harm!" Jonathon repeated incredulously. "Don't

108

you realize the delicacy of our situation? I thought I had made myself all the clear on that point."

"Yes, my lord," she told him with her hands. "But Mister Rexley arrived at my chamber door completely unannounced. I could but give him entrance to converse with me."

"That is not surprising in the least," Jonathon replied, casting his brother a scathing look.

"What is not surprising," Cyril asked indignantly. "What did she tell you?" He moved his accusing gaze to Lark. "What did you tell him?"

"Do not speak to her in that tone," Jonathon admonished blackly. "You show her the respect you would show our mother if she were standing at your side. All the better, you bestow *more* respect on my fiancée."

Lark's brows arched. It was incredulous just how much Jonathon could appear to hold her in high regard, when all the while he secretly despised her. What a heart less cad.

A heartless cad who held her own heart in captivity.

She stared at him until Cyril's chuckling drew her attention in his direction.

"I think it is best..."

"It is all my fault..."

Cyril and Rebekka began to speak in unison then both hushed. Cyril nodded in deference to the abigail. "Dragons first," he whittled playfully.

She turned to Jonathon. "It is all my doing. I foolishly allowed him entrance when I knew I should not. Please do not think ill of Miss Lark. She knows no better."

Jonathon studied the innocence of his fiancée. It emanated from her like a spiritual aura. Think ill of her? It was impossible, he was sure.

"'Tis me he thinks ill of, not she," Cyril cut in blandly. "I think it's best if I take my leave." He turned an inquiring eye to Lark. "Do you think it would be proper for me to leave you unattended in your chambers with a gentleman of my brother's character?"

When she did not reply, he shrugged and carried himself to the door. He turned to Jonathon. "I have secured Almack's for a fortnight hence when we shall all be out of black gloves." He waved offhandedly, "A party to celebrate the betrothal of my brother to the lovely Miss Lark Black—burn."

"You did no such thing!" Jonathon took steps toward his meddling brother. "Why, there are rumors circulating and you...why...*you* are the cause of all the prattle."

"Am I not always the cause of all the prattle?" Cyril sighed. "Not to worry, old chap, Lark's beauty will still the wagging tongues. Of that I have no doubt." He cast her a final look before disappearing down the corridor.

Jonathon turned back to Lark. "I apologize deeply for the waywardness of my brother. He means no harm at all."

"No harm done, my lord," she answered nobly. "He is but charming in his own incorrigible way."

"Mmm," Lord Somerset said, glancing off into nothing. "Charming indeed." He focused on his bride-to-be once more. "Not to worry, Miss Lark. I shall do all in my power to cancel these ridiculous proceedings Cyril has devised."

"Were you not planning such the thing?" she asked.

"Precisely, but I was not to do it so soon after mourning. I wished to wait a respectable period—to enhance the look of authenticity of our supposed blossoming love," he added.

"I see," she signed. "Perhaps now it would look more respectable were you not to cancel a thing."

Jonathon thought for a moment. "I suppose you're right." He sighed. "I wish for your presence in the library. Do you think you could accommodate my request presently?"

Lark curtsied, but Rebekka was the one who replied.

"Aye, my lord. She'll be there posthaste."

****

From the doorway, Lark watched Jonathon stalk back and forth across the library floor, intermittently looking to the portrait of his mother. His thought seemed so deeply imbedded that she hated to interrupt him.

Silently, she stepped into the room and padded across the large embellished carpet. His back was to her as he paced in the opposite direction. She approached him carefully, not wanting to disturb him, yet not wanting to be accused of eavesdropping again.

He twirled around and stopped abruptly. "You really do need to learn how to make some noise, Miss Lark," he said forcefully, his ragged breathing evidence to the start she had given him.

She took a step in retreat. "I apologize, my lord," she told him with her hands. "I wanted to get your attention so you would not think ill of me once again."

"For goodnes'sake! Rap on a door or some such thing. Do not sneak up on a person with cat's paws."

She cast her gaze quickly downward, embarrassed heat washing over her.

He sighed. With a step towards her, he placed a gentle hand on her shoulder. "I am forever apologizing to you, it seems. I can't remember having the need to so often humble myself."

Her eyes moved to the tender hand on her shoulder and he quickly snatched it away. Her eyes darted to his face.

He was looking at her coolly, and she wondered not for the first time if her physical appearance repulsed him as well as her handicap.

"There is no need to apologize for my deficiency. It is through no fault of yours you have been saddled with me."

Jonathon's eyebrows drew together. "Saddled with you?" He sighed and took a retreating step. "I realize I bore that attitude for a time, Miss Lark, but no longer. Never fear. I may not understand fully as yet, but I do fulfill my father's wishes with relish. It is the least I can do."

So, he was now pleased to marry her—but his desire was tainted by duty, the fulfillment of a dead man's request. It was better than nothing she supposed, but not nearly enough. She wasn't sure she could survive spending the rest of her life knowing that her marriage ranked with that of the silver and china—an inherited burden.

"I am suddenly weary," she signed. "Would you object to my sitting?"

"I seem to effectively tire you, do I not? A fact I shall have to remedy before too long. I shouldn't want you growing old before your time." She cast him a puzzled glance, and he offhandedly indicated any chair. "Do sit.

My manners fail me this day."

She made her way into the corner, her favorite chair, and sat down, smoothing her skirts quite efficiently before raising her gaze to him once more.

He watched her significantly. "Do you sit in the shadows by default or by design?" He asked.

Lark signed her reply and he sighed impatiently. "There, you see. I cannot read your speech if I cannot see your hands." He tromped over to the mantle and picked up a heavy silver candelabra. With determined steps, he trod the floor between them and removed some books on the case at her side in order to make room for the light.

She peered up at him nervously. He towered over her in the most eerie manner under the glow of the candelabra's flickering light. She closed her eyes and took a cleansing breath. This was only Jonathon.

Jonathon whom she loved.

Jonathon who would never love her in return.

She lifted her hands and repeated her former reply. "This is my favorite chair. Since I was but a child."

He smiled down at her, then. "You are still a child, my dear."

"There are mothers younger than I," she countered.

A sound escaped his throat. "Yes, but none who have not seen the world in some form or other."

He moved away from her, then, and changed the subject completely. "I must discuss a matter of great importance with you." He turned to face her once again, the width of the room a canyon between them. "Do understand that I am not seeking permission or approval, merely understanding. As my future wife, I am sure you will see fit to abide my wishes and keep this conversation in the strictest confidence."

She nodded and he began.

"I have some business to attend to and may be gone several days." He glanced at her. "This is not a problem, but my return may be difficult for you to accept."

"I do not understand," she signed.

He removed his gaze from her face and stared at his boots as he paced the floor. "If things do not go as planned, upon my return I will have a house guest—well, much more than a guest, in truth, he would be a permanent fixture."

He stopped directly in front of the fireplace and drew his hands about himself, rubbing his arms. "It grows chilly," he said. Making his way to the door, he jerked the bell pull.

Chauncy appeared promptly, sliding the doors open just enough to peer in. "Yes, milord."

"Set a fire in the hearth and bring us some tea." He glanced to Lark. "Do you prefer something besides tea?"

She shook her head and he turned back to Chauncy in silence.

"Yes, milord," Chauncy said, removing his head from the portal and gently sliding the doors closed behind him.

Jonathon smiled at Lark. "You know, you had been sitting in that very place the first time I saw you."

She nodded and cast abashed eyes downward. She did not like to think much of that day. He had accused her of eavesdropping, of deliberately hiding in the shadows like some plague-riddled rat.

"You emerged out of the shadows like a ghost." An airy quality to his voice made Lark take greater notice.

"The sconce light flickered on your face, defining the exquisite—" His eyes focused on her and he snapped closed his mouth. He cleared an obstruction in his throat. "Excuse me." He began to draw nearer the fireplace again as Chauncy came in and went about starting a fire.

It rent her heart that he found it so difficult to converse with her. Each time it seemed he would finally speak to her as an equal, share something of consequence, he checked himself.

She wanted to be a true partner to him, but she so repulsed him, he couldn't even bring himself converse with her. Yes, he had said he now wed her with relish, but not because he held her in high regard, but because it was the least he could do.

Duty. Honor. Were not these the qualities she liked about him?

Oh, how she wished responsibility would bow to love.

While the butler completed his duties, Jonathon watched in silence and did not address Lark again until they were once again in privacy. "Better," he mumbled, holding his palms out to the strengthening kindling.

"Where was I? Oh yes, I may have to bring my nephew here to raise him. There have been some recent difficulties, which I am not at liberty to discuss with you, that need my immediate attention. Geoffry shall be in need of a male to guide him to majority."

She wanted to ask questions, but he merely continued to show her his back. She sighed audibly, but he seemed too ensconced in his thoughts to notice.

"I realize you are but young to suddenly become mother to a young man of Geoffry's years, but if I cannot avoid the outcome, which I must confess, I hope does not come to pass—not because I don't love my cousin, you understand, but because I hope he is loved enough to prevent the procurement of such turn of events—but if I cannot avoid the outcome you must remain at my side in judgment as a loyal wife would." He finally found the time to breathe and halted his concourse of words.

Lark was so confused she was sure her mind would not stop spinning for a month of Sundays.

She feared he would begin again without looking to her. Thus, out of desperation, she began to beat sufficiently on the arm of the gilt chair.

At first, she didn't think even that was going to draw his attention, but as she applied more force to her plight, he turned and queried her silently.

She expelled a relieved breath and then looked at him. She was surprised by the haggard countenance expressed on his usually unaffected features. She didn't understand it, but he was truly engaged in a troublesome dilemma.

A sudden urge to comfort him enveloped her, and she quelled the impulse to close the distance between them. "Why do you tell me this? You must know I will forever be loyal to you. As you voiced, I could do no less than honor Lord Peter's wishes after all he has done for me," she signed.

He showed her a wan smile. "It's not having Geoffry here after we are wed that distresses me." He locked gazes with her. "It is the fact that if I must bring him into the home he will arrive a considerable time before we are actually married. You would have to once again become the Somerset Ghost to avoid disgrace."

With full clarity, she understood the weight of the situation. Oh, she could not remain locked in chambers again. She just couldn't. She would not have a wit remaining.

"I understand the difficulty, and perhaps it shall not come to such a drastic measure. I merely wished for you to be prepared rather than surprise you with such dreadful news in the event it should become necessity. Of course, this whole Almack's thing has set plans in a tither, but that can't be helped now. Zounds! Cyril must have been in fine twig to arrange this to-do."

"I cannot," she signed simply. "It was—"

She was interrupted by the arrival of Penelope and a cart of tea and tarts. "I thought ye might like a light bite with your tea, my lord," she said cheerily as she poured milk into both cups before scalding it with the freshly steeped, golden liquid.

Lark sat rigidly in the chair until the housemaid had completed her task, the words she had been about to express, still tingling her fingertips. As Penelope took her leave, Lark turned her attention to her fiancé.

"Before, when Lord Peter's will was pronounced, I found it best difficult to remain in my chambers for a fortnight. Please understand, my lord," she quickly explained, as his look grew black. "While Lord Peter lived, he kept visitors at bay on the whole, and during those rare occasions he did entertain, I could stand to be discreet for a few hours." She hoped he understood; she just could not do that again.

She studied him, and watched as his black expression softened. He closed the distance between them, bent one knee, and knelt at her side. He took her hand in both of his and gazed solemnly into her face. His hands, encasing hers, were warm from the fire and heated her through and through. She smiled at him.

"I understand the difficulty. I would not ask of you anything so harsh if there were another alternative."

He gazed directly into her eyes, silently imploring her to understand, and it melted every objection she had in her head. How could she refuse him, he looked so needy...and charming...and handsome.

He patted her hand. "And perhaps this will not come

to pass." He smiled a smile rife with boyish charm and mischief. "I have devised quite a plan."

Chapter Sixteen

Lady Wescotte was adorned in a Coburg walking dress, the likes of which Jonathon had never before seen. As he entered the vestibule, she already awaited, slipping into kid gloves so large several animals must have been sacrificed in the making. They matched the expressive emerald dress without flaw and Jonathon was forced to admit that his dragon of a relative actually looked quite presentable.

"I must express my surprise at seeing you so prompt this morning, Aunt Harriet," he told her as Simpson took his quiet leave.

She grunted a reply. "I merely want this business over with, you impertinent boy."

Jonathon forced the corners of his lips to remain even. "Where, pray tell, is the young Geoffry?"

She shook her head. "I told the lad to make haste. Better, you be off with him. You will see the difficulties a boy can bring." She eyed him carefully. "Have you not discussed this matter with your future fiancée? She will no doubt become completely rag-mannered at the prospect." Jonathon didn't miss the air of triumph in her tone, although he chose to ignore it in deference to carrying out his plans.

"Truth be out, I have discussed it with Miss Lark, however, I daresay, it is not her place to disobey my wishes. I am quite happy to inform you she was not overset in the least. In fact, she was the pattern card of grace and understanding."

He took a step toward his aunt. "Of course, I didn't tell her the *entire* truth, you understand. And I do not intend to allow Geoffry knowledge of his parentage. I will merely extend him an invitation into my home. Is that clearly understood?"

"Of course I understand. I no more wish to cast

117

Geoffry into the briars than do you. Why, it wouldn't do us much good either."

Geoffry came then, clattering in a manner most unbecoming of a gentleman. "My apologies for keeping you waiting, Mama." He gave a smile to Lord Somerset. "Jonathon."

"Cabbage head!" Lady Wescotte rebuked.

Jonathon frowned. The thought crossed his mind that perhaps he should do away with his deception and actually take the boy Aunt Harriet was forever oversetting the poor lad. It was true Geoffry was a bit bumbling, but nothing that couldn't be cured by a little praise and confidence.

Geoffry subdued considerably then a smile came across his crooked lips and excitement boiled behind his eyes. "Mama says you are to take us on a special carriage ride this morning?"

"That's correct. I have a matter of great importance to discuss with you."

Geoffry beamed with enthusiasm. "Shall we take our leave, then?" Hurriedly, he shrugged into an overcoat that seemed all at once to swallow him up.

Good Heavens, Jonathon thought, *the lad needs to be plumped like a Christmas goose.*

Without further delay, Jonathon helped Lady Wescotte struggle into the dogcart, and their journey began. She sat very quietly, watching the familiar scenery pass along, but it was not an uncomfortable silence. On the contrary, Jonathon was quite pleased that she'd decided against any flapdoodle to fill the silence.

Geoffry, of course, remained his generally subdued self, thus Jonathon was left with his musings to fill the empty chambers in his head.

When they had been traveling a considerable time, Lady Wescotte broke the silence. "Do you have a particular destination, or were you going to jostle me until I turned up my toes."

"My, you are a dreadful grouser this morning, are you not?" Jonathon did not cast his eyes in her direction.

"I am not such a thing," Lady Wescotte shot back, her double chins flapping with the indignant snort that came up her throat and out her nose. "And you are a cad! The manners I hear bragged about have dissolved before my very eyes. You are no better than that wastrel brother of yours."

Jonathon glanced back at Geoffry. "What say you of this trip, dear boy? Are you breathless for its end?"

Geoffry's face paled as his eyes darted between his mother and his cousin. It was most apparent he feared his opinion might prove to offend one or the other of them.

Lady Wescotte turned a triumphant eye to Jonathon at the precise moment he chose to look at her. He quickly returned his gaze to the horses and the lane ahead. Geoffry never quite answered the query, and Jonathon did not press the situation.

They reached a secluded spot rich in grasses and wildflowers and Jonathon brought the horses to a stop. Climbing down from the carriage, he helped Lady Wescotte to the ground. "There you are, Aunt Harriet, a wonderful place for you to cure your aches and pains."

"I have most definitely come down with a case of the megrims."

"Nothing a little fresh air won't cure. Why don't you sit in the shade of that tree? There is a bench, and Geoffry and I shall exercise our legs and empty the bag."

Lady Wescotte's eyes darted to his face and transfixed themselves there. "You wish to speak to Geoffry without me present?"

"Why, Aunt Harriet, surely you must know I collected you as a courtesy. If Uncle Wescotte were not indisposed, 'twould be he who would make the decision after Geoffry any way."

"Please, allow me to accompany the two of you. Geoffry is used to having some guidance in such matters."

Jonathon studied his aunt's uneasy expression. It relieved him to notice that she really didn't want to lose Geoffry—yet her pride still would not let her voice such. He took pity on her.

"Come, Geoffry. We are to walk a bit," Jonathon said.

The boy bustled to them, taking his mother's arm like a gentleman. "Do tell, Jonathon, what is this pressing matter you wished to discuss with *me*?" Geoffry's voice squeaked, and Jonathon realized anew, just how young and inexperienced the boy was.

119

Jonathon glanced at Lady Wescotte. She looked ahead stoically, seeming to ignore them both. He smiled. Maybe she wasn't such a dragon, after all. The breeze picked up, and he felt the chill. For a brief moment, he wondered if he should torture his aunt so. She may have played a heartless card, but wasn't this plan of his a trifle cruel in itself?

Pressing onward, he looked to Geoffry. "I have taken over my father's estate, as you well know, and soon I will be taking a wife. I have discussed it with your mother, and she and I believe that it would be best if you were to come to Somerset Manor and reside there until your majority."

The boy's face lost all trace of color with the exception of the maroon tinge that darkened his thin lips. His arm fell away from that of his mother's, and his steps halted so abruptly, he was left behind before Jonathon or Aunt Harriett could think to wait. For several seconds, Jonathon truly thought Geoffry was going to expire.

Now, as they stood strides in front of him, turned around and staring back at the boy, Jonathon noted the concern etched on his aunt's face like the immovable smile on the face of the *Mona Lisa*, and realized at once that her countenance portrayed the same knot that had tightened in his own chest.

"Geoffry?" Jonathon prodded. He took a step toward the boy and Geoffry countered with a backwards step of his own. Jonathon stopped, held out a hand to him. "Geoffry, are you quite the thing?"

Geoffry's dead eyes were glazed over, his gaze transfixed on his statue of a mother. That woman suddenly moved like lightening to come to stand beside her son. Jonathon was not only taken aback by her quickness, but also by her agility—and her concern. He knew instantly this was not a game he should have played.

"Speak to me this instant," she instructed Geoffry harshly.

His voice cracked. "Is it the truth that you wish for me to live with my cousins?" His forlorn gaze penetrated his mother's face. "I know I have always been a disappointment to you, Mama, but I did not expect to be expelled."

Jonathon's insides crumbled. He had been so enthralled by his spark of genius that he had failed miserably to see the larger picture. He had been of mind only of the proposed thoughts and actions of Aunt Harriet. Not once had he thought about the effects his plans would have on his cousin—in truth, his own half-brother.

Guilt and remorse packed his stomach with lead. He, above all, should have been able to see what his plan would do to Geoffry. After all, he himself had been ousted from his family home, rejected by his papa. It was most damaging to one's stamina. He'd certainly struggled with similar woes, and he had never been as delicate as Geoffry.

In all his mind, he would have never thought himself capable of inflicting such circumstance on someone else.

Lady Wescotte's reply filtered into Jonathon's mind.

"To be true, I thought Jonathon was much too inexperienced to do justice by you," she said, and then she did something Jonathon had never been witness to before. She lifted her gloved arms and engaged Geoffry in the most motherly of embraces. "I would not change you for all the world, my dear," she told him sincerely.

Jonathon had never hoped to see such a display of affection from his codfish of an aunt, and emotion rose, unbidden, into his heart. He approached them, and Harriett drew herself away from Geoffry. When Jonathon set eyes once again on his nephew, the boy's eyes were missishly soupy.

Jonathon ignored it. He came to stand directly in front of the lad, all the while, well aware of the vicious stare being projected from the general vicinity of his aunt. "I apologize profusely, Geoffry." he bowed politely. "I must admit, I devised bird-witted plan. I did not think past the lesson I wished Au—*someone*—to learn."

"I don't understand at all," Geoffry said.

"Nor could you be expected to," Jonathon replied. "Remember this: when you love someone, do not risk losing them for anything in this world." He glanced at his aunt, who, for all her sympathy earlier, was now returned to the dour-puss she seemingly enjoyed most of all.

"You speak nonsense to confuse the boy," she spat. "Do you think we could call this absurdity over and return to the luxuries of home?"

He eyed her knowingly. "That's entirely up to you," he said evenly.

She sighed. "Your father, my brother—rest his soul—is gone. I daresay, whatever dies with him, dies with him."

"*I* daresay that is an excellent observation, Aunt Harriet." Jonathon swiveled his head back to Geoffry. "What's say I treat some of my most beloved relatives to ices at Gunter's?"

"Well it—" Lady Wescotte began to object before she caught the warning glance from Jonathon. Her eyes moved to Geoffry who looked completely overdone.

"I am all agog for Gunter's," she amended.

Chapter Seventeen

"You look exquisite, my lady," Rebekka told Lark as they stood, side by side in front of the full length looking glass.

Lark had to agree despite her initial objection to the revealing décolletage of the new evening gown. The additional flesh exposed by the low neckline caused her to look a great deal more sophisticated than the modest shifts she was used to. The bouffant sleeves puffed out gracefully at her shoulders and caused her waist to appear even smaller than the normal entrappings of stays. And the color the mantuamaker incorporated into the embroidery of the white ivory gown enhanced her pale complexion more than she had believed possible. In truth, she had never given the color of her skin much mind until now. The pastel green and lavender carried through onto the silk cartage cymar highlighted every contour of her body in a way she never dreamed.

She twisted this way, then that, to view the rear of her dress—a flowing train adorned by the silk scarf. She glanced again in the mirror to the reflection of Rebekka. "I do appear to look quite a lady, do I not?"

"Aye," Rebekka, agreed with relish.

"Do you suppose Lord Somerset will be pleased?" She wanted so to please him above all else. She had seen little of him this fortnight passed and now she was off to a betrothal ball—not *a* betrothal ball, *her* betrothal ball—to be held at one of the most prestigious establishments in all of England. Her insides refused to settle. Her mind whirred with the lessons she had endured these six months past—how to dance, how to use one's fan, how to engage in conversation—something she was over-positive she would not have to engage in once the *ton* discovered her inability for speech.

Mindfully she went through the steps of the quadrille

and the waltz, pictured fashions and recalled their names, brought forth the recollections of all the prominent names in society.

Her delicate confidence crumbled. There was entirely too much information for one person to remember.

"Are you all the thing, Miss Lark?"

"I am but a bowl of rotten fruit!" Lark wailed with flamboyant fingers.

Rebekka chuckled.

"You think it is funny?"

"Not at all, my lady," Rebekka bubbled between chortles.

"Well, I assure you it is not funny in the least. I'm about to meet society in the most intimate way and do a bang up job of humiliating myself. Not to mention Jon— Lord Somerset," she signed with vigorous gestures.

Rebekka regained control of her laughter and lovingly patted Lark on the back. "Do you not think you could speak? If you could bring yourself to this I know your confidence would grow."

Lark sighed. "Haven't we had this conversation before? Do you think that if I had the power to be normal for my lord I would do it not?"

Rebekka appeared rightly chastised. "No," she answered softly. "I am sure that if it were in your power you would do him up proud." She moved to the dressing table. "'Tis almost time. We had best get your gloves on. And, do allow me to check your bonnet once more for security."

Lark took one last look in the mirror at the babet covering her ears and the back of her head. She was more inclined to prefer flowers arranged in her hair, but she supposed this would do.

"Come on, then. Cheer up that long face. This is your come-out, Miss. Treat it as such and you shall have not a care in the world."

Lark began her way to the dressing table and allowed Rebekka to adjust the hat. "This is an engagement to-do, not a come-out. Were it a come-out I would have all the excitement of finding a suitable match."

Rebekka scoffed. "You don't call Lord Somerset a

suitable match? You must've gone round the bend! Think yourself lucky, my gel; you don't have to parade yourself in hopes of making a match like other girls your age. You can be set in the fact that you have already secured a sought-after suitor. You will be the envy of all."

"The envy of all, or the envy of all those who are themselves deficient?"

"We are all deficient in something," Rebekka told her outright. "Take me, for instance. I am not a proficient reader, yet, after taking my learnings and passing them on to you, you have well surpassed my ability."

"Forgive me, Rebekka, but you are a servant. I am not going to be judged by the same standards that you are judged. As a lady I will be expected to be perfect."

"You most certainly have grown up this ha'year past," Rebekka observed wistfully. "I daresay I preferred you full of innocence rather than vinegar."

"I am not full of vinegar!" Lark signed wildly. "I am—"

"Still yourself, before you get a head full of pins!"

Lark quieted and allowed Rebekka to finish securing the bonnet to her head. "I am merely realistic," Lark finished when Rebekka had completed her task.

Rebekka picked up one glove from the dressing table and motioned for Lark to hold out her arm. "I will not lie to you, as I never have. This night will be frightful. It is the most important night of your life, thus far. But you will be better served by remaining calm and confident rather than allowing your fears and the vultures of the *ton* to best you." She finished applying the glove to Lark's hand and began with the next one.

"Remember, I am all for you and will be at your side, as will Lord Somerset, and I daresay, Master Cyril. That outlandish gentleman has the best in mind for you just as well as Lord Somerset. You are blessed to be so well taken care of. Relax and be thankful, not rancid."

Lark sighed. She could do nothing else since her hands were being attended. Perhaps Rebekka was right. Perhaps she would be better served by meeting the *ton* with an air of confidence rather than shriveling into a corner and disappearing behind a potted plant.

She had spent the better part of the last six months

wondering if she could make Jonathon love her, if she could get through their betrothal and subsequent marriage without disgracing everything he was. Now, tonight, all her fears were piled like a barrel full of snow in winter. And how would it end? She was unsure.

Smiling at Rebekka's reflection, she took a cleansing breath and pulled herself out of the chair. "Do you suppose Lord Somerset awaits? I haven't seen him since this morning, and then it was but in passing."

"I'm sure he awaits you anxiously, my lady. And so does the rest of the *ton*." Rebekka smiled and picked off a remnant of lint from the bodice of Lark's gown. "We're ready, I do believe."

Lark rewarded her abigail with a beautiful smile full of hope. She would enter society with confidence. She only hoped it didn't flee once she was announced.

****

Dread filled Jonathon. He couldn't remember being so utterly out of sorts since the first time he had confronted a member of Society after his father removed him from the house. He paced laboriously the length of his chamber.

He pulled out his pocket watch and took note of the time. Lark should be ready to take her leave. He wondered if she were as nervous as he. He was sure she must be—more so, perhaps. He had wanted to speak to her these days past but had neither the time, nor the courage, to do so. He was still perturbed at himself over the mess he had made with his scheme to teach Aunt Harriet a lesson. And that did not mingle well with his growing agitation at the lack of facts Hollingsworth had been able to uncover regarding Lark's past.

Jonathon let out a growl. He was a damned fool and needed to rethink all his motivations of late. He had completely overset young Geoffry without even considering the possibility, and neither could he find any cause in Lark's past for her to be in danger. For all his attempts, he was no good to anybody.

He sighed and picked up his riding gloves before taking his leave of the room. He desperately prayed he could pull off the evening's charade. If they were all to escape scandal, it was imperative that all partygoers believe whole-heartedly he and Lark had been courting long before his father's death. If there were even a hint that he had not mourned sufficiently these past six months, it would be the end of them all.

When he made it below stairs and waited in the study for Lark to ready herself. She took a veritable age, and he wondered if it were because she was a woman, or because she wanted to stall.

Finally, a rap came at the door, and Lark entered with Rebekka trailing behind. He looked up from his brandy and was struck speechless. Her smile undid him to the full, and his tough wall of defenses crumbled within him. He closed his eyes and opened them slowly.

"Good evening, Miss Lark. You are an exceptionally pink picture," he managed to get past his dry throat. "I daresay you will steal the ball."

She politely bent a knee and bestowed on him an even larger smile. "You are most kind," she signed.

For a brief moment, Lark was glad of the fact that she was unable to speak for had she been expected to reply, she would surely have said something to disgrace herself.

At her first vision of Jonathon in formalwear, she was taken completely unaware by the responsive way her body reacted. In truth, she was not completely positive exactly what she experienced. Her stomach was overcome with flutterings, and her heartbeat pounded so loudly, she was afraid Jonathon might hear it.

His tan pantaloons molded especially to his well-muscled legs, and upon noticing such, Lark felt the heat of blush rise up her neck. What, should he guess her reaction to such observation—or that she had such observation at all?

The snug cut of his coat served to emphasize the broadness of his shoulders, and as the gilt buttons down the front caught the lamp light, Lark couldn't help but notice the expanse of his hard chest. She quickly averted her eyes.

"You are ready to depart?" His words brought back Lark's mind, and her eyes, once again, found the courage to seek him. She nodded, tentatively at the onset, then more pronounced as she realized it would do no good to appear over-nervous.

"Very well." His eyes moved to Rebekka who stood silently behind her miss. "Go and confirm that the carriage awaits. Miss Lark and I shall meet you outside in a trice."

"But—"

"Don't mention formalities in this house, Rebekka. You can resume your watch over Miss Lark as soon as we are arrived at Almack's. For now, act as you have for months past."

"Yes, my lord," Rebekka replied obediently, although Lark heard her mumbling something unintelligible as she took her leave.

Jonathon approached Lark. "So, are your nerves atwitter?" He smiled at her and the birds took flight in her stomach again.

"Not at all," she replied with her hands.

He laughed outright. "You are not a very good liar, Miss Lark. Even without a voice to betray you, your eyes speak volumes mere words never could." He took her hand in his own and star down at where they were joined for several moments before he spoke. "We have been quite scandalous here at home. I have become quite accustomed to speaking to you without chaperon, to being able to take your hand when those eyes of yours look as if you need comfort. It is going to be best difficult to remember proprieties while we are with other people." His gaze rose to hers. "You have spoiled me."

Lark did not know how to react. She stared at him, dazed, her mind full of nothing, yet everything. She couldn't remember experiencing more joy, or more confusion in all her days. Finally, she forced a smile, and that seemed to satisfy him.

"Let us go, then, shall we?" He left her momentarily to retrieve his chapeau bras, then slipped her hand over his arm and escorted her to the carriage where Rebekka and the groom were already waiting.

The pageantry was greater than any vision Lark could have imagined. As they entered the famous assembly rooms on King's Street, St. James, a bolster of activity greeted them. If she had been one of speech, she surely would have been struck dumb with the carriage ride into the heart of London and the equipage that carried them there in such luxury. But even that was not as lavish as the elegant eveningwear of both the ladies and the gentlemen. She did not even take exception to the bland decoration of the hall.

Upon their entrance, Cyril dashed over immediately. He offered his hand to Jonathon and they greeted each other in silence. Cyril then turned his eyes to Lark and grinned at her most mischievously. He bent at the waist slightly. "Good evening, Miss Lark. It is a pleasure to see you again," he said formally. Lark was taken quite aback by his manner; she hadn't thought it possible for the most outspoken Mr. Rexley to be subdued.

She feared this was only the first of many surprises she would have to endure before the evening expired.

She curled the corners of her lips in a gracious salute and, to her incredulity, Cyril leaned closer to her ear. "Don't be afraid," he said. "I shan't let the vultures devour you."

He withdrew from her and she glanced to her side at Jonathon. The crease in his frowning brow and the manner in which he shot daggers with his eyes at the retreating Mister Rexley told her he was not a little overset. "I shall have a word with him before the cock crows," he mumbled blackly. He moved his gaze to Lark. "I must apologize for my brother's lack of manners. He is too much."

He scanned the occupants of the room. "This eve should be kindly done," he said, causing Lark much puzzlement. He smiled down at her. "Would you like a refreshment?"

She nodded, more out of courtesy than of a true need for something refreshing. She took time to scan the room and pointed to an unoccupied spot in a near corner. She hoped he understood her meaning, for she wished to avoid using her hands.

"Don't be afraid," he said in low tones, and she wondered for a moment if he had heard his brother's words. Not wanting to ask, she just stared at him until he left her for the refreshments bar.

She and Rebekka made their way unheeded to the neutral corner that Lark hoped would serve to protect her from too much introduction.

Before any time had passed, an elegantly dressed young miss and an older woman approached Lark. The elder of the two, whose graying hair was topped with a bonnet of plumes the breadth of which Lark had never seen, greeted her with a smile. "I am the Marchioness of Abberley. May I present my daughter, Margaret."

Lark smiled warmly hoping that the small gesture would appease the marchioness and the ladies would take their leave. She was, however, largely disappointed. She wrung her gloved hands while her mind whirred with what to do next, when the young Miss Margaret spoke.

"This is such a wonderful party. Mister Rexley did a bang up job on the..." She broke off her sentence at the sharp look of her mother.

The Marichioness's gaze softened as she focused once more on Lark. "My daughter is but a child yet to make her come-out. Her manners slip."

Lark could not tell where the girl's manners had slipped. It had sounded more as if she were of a mind to offer a compliment. Lark's heart constricted. She had so much to learn, she was certain she would bungle the job and cause Jonathon to be a laughing stock.

A silence stretched between the three ladies until finally a subject was broached that Lark could neither ignore, nor answer with silent smiles and nods.

"I wished to reassure you we do not listen to gossipy rumors considering your betrothal to Lord Somerset. Mr. Rexley informed all that you are not formally announced and that yourself and Lord Somerset were well acquainted before the late Lord Peter breathed his last. Rest his soul." The marchioness glanced heavenward momentarily, and, unbidden, Lark's eyes followed that movement.

"Your gown is quite becoming. Praytell from which mantuamaker did you procure it?" The marchioness changed subjects as easily as one would discard a morning gown in the afternoon.

Lark swallowed hard and glanced at Rebekka for help. Rebekka raised an eyebrow in as much to say, "you cannot hide forever," and Lark responded by answering the Marchioness of Abberley with her hands.

The older lady immediately took a retreating step, staring at Lark's moving hands as if they were snakes upon Medusa's head. Lark's movements slowed until they were completely ceased.

Rebekka began to translate. "I say, your gown is exquisite itself. Surely you do not seek a re ...place ... ment ...for ... your...."

The marchioness's brown eyes grew large and her mouth fell open so wide Lark feared the woman's bottom lip would graze the floor. Her lips fluttered erratically until the top one finally stilled and allowed the bottom to quiver alone.

"W—we, we must, we must, must circulate," she stammered. Taking a firm grip on her daughter's arm, she led away the girl in haste. Lark heard her say, "The chatter was not all mistaken."

Lark inhaled a considerable breath and held it as if it might be her last. She squeezed her eyes closed, willing the biting tears to dry and the marchioness's horrified countenance to be wiped free of her mind's eye. Her efforts, save for in the matter of tears, were in vain.

She let out her breath, but found she was still living the nightmare. She wished nothing more than to flee the awful place before the Marchioness of Abberley had the notion to tell everyone of the unfortunate circumstance.

Lark shook her head; she could not rid herself of the remembrance of the Marchioness's bulging eyes. She turned her eye to Rebekka only when the abigail placed a hand on her shoulder.

"Are you fine?" Rebekka queried, obviously a little overset herself.

Lark nodded. It wasn't as if she hadn't expected this type of reception. It was more that, even though she had expected it, it wasn't quite the same as actually experiencing it.

Her eyes roamed the room in search of Jonathon. She had every confidence that were he at her side, such coarseness would not occur. She found him engaged in conversation, an expanse of room separating them as impenetrable as the English Channel. He deftly held a glass of something in one hand and a small plate of hors d'oeuvres in the other. As a servant walked by she noticed him place the glass on the tray.

****

The crystal clicked on the silver tray as Jonathon replaced the flute. He was in high dudgeon. He had observed Lark and the pretentious Marchioness of Abberley, and had witnessed Lark's complexion grow pale, her face grow stiff. He wanted nothing more than to close the distance that lay between them, but four of his so-called acquaintances were keeping him at bay with their myriad questions and prattle.

He turned his attention back to Sean McGillicuty, a Scottish earl of questionable scruples when taking into consideration the rash of ladies he courted and discarded. He was not a handsome man but had a considerable fortune to which all the ladies seemed to flock.

McGillicuty neither wondered, nor cared about any of them, and Jonathon thought that the man was a complete cad. Now the Scot had turned his attentions to Lark, Jonathon not only thought the man a cad, but also a marksman's target as well.

"She's a pink lass, that one," he was saying, his back to Lark, but evidently knowledgeable regarding her appearance from the invisible eyes in the back of his head.

Jonathon nodded absently, growing more peevish with each word McGillicuty uttered.

"Aye, I winna mind finding myself a lass who donned so pretty a face ever' morn."

Jonathon shot him a black look. "Your manners are outside of enough, McGillicuty. I shall have you know that I intend to declare myself to the fair Miss Lark, and if you do not cease this infernal smearing of her virtuous nature I shall be forced to call you out."

McGillicuty's round, freckled face momentarily went like a stone, but without much delay, he boomed a laugh that could be heard over the entire room. Eyes turned to briefly attend the huddle of men, and molten anger billowed through Jonathon with renewed intensity.

He looked at another of his acquaintance, Roger Whitman, a respectable gentleman. "Keep this man away from me for the rest of the evening, else I fear I shall do us all an injustice." His wrathful glare moved to

McGillicuty. "Well, not *all*," he added ominously, "for *some* it will be justice." He returned to a polite tone. "If you gentlemen will excuse me, I have a lady to attend."

He stormed off, and began his journey back to Lark. He was but a quarter-way across the room when the Lord and Lady of Putnumshire stopped him in mid-stride.

"This is a lovely soirée, Lord Somerset," the lady said.

"Indeed," her husband replied. "I say, do you plan to attend Tatt's on the morrow?"

Jonathon was absently staring at Putnumshire's sideburns. He did not know why they drew his attention, save for the fact that he supposed they were a new addition to the lord's countenance.

"...well-bred stallion."

Jonathon realized at once that he had missed Putnumshire's conversation completely. "I beg your pardon, but I must get these lovely refreshments to Miss Lark Blackburn." He nodded and bestowed the elderly Lady Putnumshire with a broad smile. "Hope to see you at Tatt's presently," he said absently to Lord Putnumshire, then hurried off, leaving them staring after him.

Cyril approached him next. "Saw you over there with McGillicuty. Thought you didn't care for him."

Jonathon threw Cyril a scathing look. "I do not care for him! My next obvious query being, why did you extend him an invitation?"

Cyril shrugged and looked at Jonathon with arched brows. "I couldn't very well exclude the wealthiest earl in Scotland, could I? That just would not do. Look at Lady Cowper over there," he pointed with a flick of his head in the direction of the entry. "What would she and Lady Jersey say were we to retain Almack's and not have the guest list just so?"

"Perhaps you should have thought twice about holding this nonsensical ball in the first place. We are just out of mourning and completed the task so well. You just had to start the prattle-mongers off again, didn't you?"

"I assure you, I thought of this not only twice, but several times while devising the plan."

"The plan for what!" Jonathon's voice rose in

frustration and he quickly softened it as he noticed the attention it drew. "Plan for what?" he repeated civilly.

"For introducing Lark into society, giving you the opportunity to do her up grand."

Jonathon's hackles calmed. He shook his head slowly and looked at his meddling brother in resignation. "You truly amaze me at times, Cyril," he said simply.

Cyril beamed boyishly. "Thank you," he replied before leaving Jonathon to his own devices.

The music began and Jonathon thought that finally he would be left alone long enough to return to Lark without further interruption. As couples joined the quadrille, Jonathon made his way along the periphery of the dancers.

Focusing on the dancing as he closed the gap between himself and Lark, he was forced to a halt by a voice almost directly at his ear. Jonathon's attention jolted to the man in front of him.

Nigel Aubury.

Nigel Aubury, Duke of Uttington, and current heir resident of Blackwell House, was a pudgy man, short like that French menace, Napoleon. His eyes were an odd color green, and when he looked at you, Jonathon had always thought, they took on a watery sheen that left one wondering whether or not he was on the brink of girlish tears. To enhance reasons to avoid the duke, he had an annoying habit of conversing in sentences that were not complete, and one had to be quick-witted to follow his thought patterns.

Jonathon felt a little sympathy for the man. He had no family left—save for Lark, Jonathon mentally amended—and he was such an odd-looking man, liking him came with difficulty.

This night, Jonathon bestowed Aubury with a sincere smile. "Good evening."

"Old chap. Extend my condolences. Apologies for not attending the funeral. Had business to attend. Care to introduce me to your lovely lady? Maid looks familiar. Don't s'pose you know from whence she came? Where did you meet the lady?" He sniffed considerably, pulled out a handkerchief, and began rubbing his bulbous nose with vigor then stuffed the silk back into its pocket with a wide, hairy hand. "Dratted cold. Happens all the time. What say you? Introduce me or must I seek out Rexley?" He chuckled as if he were funny as the court jester.

Jonathon did not laugh. The music was drawing to a close and he wanted to reach Lark before a throng of people distracted him once again.

"Come along," he told Aubury, "I shall introduce you to the lady." He inched his way past the rotund gentleman and said prayers silently that he might be successful in reaching his betrothed without further delay.

At his side, Aubury chatted away about nothing in particular and everything of inconsequence. Jonathon had neither the mind nor the inclination to decipher the man's prattle.

He caught Lark's attention as he neared, and he could see the obvious relief in her eyes the moment his gaze locked with hers. Remorse flooded him for having left her alone at the onset. He should have had more sense, should have been more understanding of her situation. She must feel quite like a duck without a pond, and he had left her to her own devices. He deserved to be scourged—and Cyril, too, for that matter. After all, *he* was responsible for this entire loathsome evening.

"Known the lady long? Six months over, for sure."

Jonathon ignored the question, having grown quite tired of it. It seemed the occupants of this room were more interested in how long he and Lark had been acquainted than they were of whether or not they intended to be wed. He supposed, thoroughly provoked, they had already made up their minds regarding the latter and now they needed the other morsel of information in order to sweeten the succulence of the gossip.

Chapter Eighteen

Lark watched as Jonathon and another gentleman approached. Even at a distance, a strange sense of déjà vu overcame her when she looked into the man's odd eyes, but it was not something so solid her mind dwelled upon it. Her emotions were in such upheaval that anything might set her mind to creating illusions.

She flashed Jonathon a stiff smile as an overwhelming sensation of abandonment washed over her. He shouldn't have left her alone. Didn't he understand that? A mixture of anger, hurt and fear mottled inside, and she was unaware of which emotion would take over when at last he arrived.

He came to stand directly in front of her, and handing her the plate of refreshments, returned her emotionless smile. "I am pleased to introduce Nigel Aubury, Duke of Uttington, and..."

His voice trailed off as a stomach-wrenching thought crossed his mind. He had only before thought of *others* recognizing *Lark*, it had never entered his mind that *she* may remember someone, and thus so, expose herself to dangers he had yet to uncover himself.

Panic seized him. He hoped Lark had no recognition of the man who had claimed her rightful inheritance by default, and if she did not recollect Aubury, Jonathon did not want his own action to give away the game. He schooled himself to remain outwardly aloof.

He chanced a glance at Rebekka. She stood as stiff as a corpse. Her eyes had narrowed to barely open slits and she studied Aubury with scarcely concealed contempt. Jonathon issued another silent prayer.

Aubury took Lark's extended free hand and bowed over her glove. "Pleasure to meet you Miss Blackburn. Rare beauty you are. Truly lovely." He turned his attention, most interestedly, to Rebekka but did not address her.

Lark gave him a polite smile, then thrust the plate of refreshments back at Jonathon and answered the Duke of Uttington with her hands. Jonathon's quick reflexes were all that saved the plate from smashing to the floor.

"I am happy to make your acquaintance," Rebekka translated.

Aubury's eyes darted from the young miss to the abigail and finally came to rest on Jonathon. "Want to explain?"

Jonathon did not. Yet, despite his reluctance, knew it was necessary. "Miss Blackburn is unable to speak at the moment. She relays messages with a language she acquired at a very young age." To demonstrate his skill at this language, he thrust the refreshments plate to Rebekka and signed to Lark all he did not want her to reveal.

"Remember my father's wishes. If you encounter anyone from your past—your past before you came to live at Somerset Manor, please do not reveal knowledge of them. If we are to play out this charade, it must be done with utmost accuracy."

"You speak in riddles," Lark told him with her hands. She turned to Rebekka. "He speaks in riddles," she repeated.

Rebekka's eyes grew worried. She shook her head. "No," she said aloud, simply.

"Trust me," Jonathon signed to Lark, and then turned to Aubury. "As Miss Blackburn and I are long acquaintances I have learned to use her language. If there is something she would like to say to you, either I or Rebekka, here, will be able to interpret."

Aubury cast a darkened glance at Rebekka once again. "Not necessary," he said. He moved his green, aqueous, eyes to Lark. "Must take my leave. Lovely making acquaintance." He bowed politely and began to back away. "Hope to see you."

With that, he bade a hasty retreat and Lark found the plate of refreshments handed to her once again. She stared at it as if it were a battalion of foreign soldiers come to arrest her.

She hadn't wished to be confined to her quiet

quarters so much in all her days. Absently, she picked at the food on the plate. Her stomach protested as the stale cake staked its claim. Without thought for propriety, her nose wrinkled at the awful taste, and she thrust the plate back at Jonathon with vengeful force. What was she doing here? She did not belong here any more than a marketeer from a London street. She might be a Lady by birth, but she was no closer to the *ton* in upbringing than a commoner.

And neither was she close to attaining the perfection expected of Society.

She swallowed hard, fighting back the urge to weep. Jonathon had been right about one thing. This was a charade. And charades was a game at which she was not proficient, especially when the stakes ran so high. This was life, and everything was on the line.

Something mentally snapped and a quiet calm washed over her. She was wrong. Nothing was on the line. The life of which she had become accustomed had died six months ago with Lord Peter. She had nothing. Nothing in the least.

She glanced up and looked directly into Jonathon's eyes.

"I know the food is not quite appetizing," he said. "But we'll dine in a short time, and I'll make sure the dinner dance belongs to me," he told her brightly.

He spoke of dining and dancing as if all were the picture of rightness. He didn't understand her at all.

He smiled. "I am sorry for the delay in returning to you. As I think you noticed, some acquaintances engaged me in conversation and I was hard-pressed to escape."

"It is quite all right," she answered politely. And it was. There was nothing he could do to make the evening any better. She just needed to escape.

"I saw the Marichioness and her daughter approach you. She was polite, was she not?"

"Of course," Lark replied, but she caught Rebekka shaking her head in a slow negative reply.

Lark shot Rebekka a warning glance full of admonition.

Rebekka shrugged and resumed her pretense of indifference.

"I am glad to hear it. I wish I could say the same about my cronies." He came to stand beside Lark.

"You see that slight gentleman, there, behind Cyril?" She nodded once she had located him, and Jonathon continued. "He is somehow related to Lady Jersey, or so the story is told."

Lark was sure this was supposed to transport her to a place of awe, but Lady Jersey was really just a name to her—one that was thrown about with reverence, but still just a name.

She smiled and tried to look interested. The music began again and ladies and gentlemen paired off, filling the dance floor with spirals of colour. Lark's heart filled with a hopeless mixture of envy and fright. She wanted to dance with her Lord Somerset, to feel his palm against her own in a waltz, yet not here, but rather at home, where she was comfortable and could mash his toes without making a fool of herself.

She chanced a look at him and her gaze held his. Moments stretched between them, and she wondered what he was thinking behind those hooded eyes. At last, he smiled, and she was once again at ease.

"Would you care to fill your dance card, this evening, Miss Lark?"

She smiled hesitantly and was about to reply when Cyril interrupted them. "Now, now. No monopolies on the fair Miss Lark, Jon. I should like to have a go around the dance floor with her." He turned to Lark and proffered a hand. "Perhaps you would grant me the next quadrille?"

"You are tiresome, Cyril," Jonathon told his brother without sign of remorse.

"I am merely trying to make Miss Lark feel at home," he said, and then added with a grin, "and save her dainty toes from being crushed under your clobbering feet." His eyes moved to Lark. "Terrible dancer, my brother," he said cheerfully.

Lark shook her head in adamant protest and signed such a hasty reply that even Jonathon looked to Rebekka for translation.

"Miss Lark says Lord Somerset is an excellent dancer."

Jonathon's lips curved into a wide smile. "There you

have it, Cyril. I am an excellent dancer." He bowed his head in Lark's direction. "Thank you."

Cyril quirked an eyebrow at his brother. "And just how would Miss Lark know how well you move your feet?"

Jonathon was stopped cold by that pointed inquiry, and did not recover for several seconds. Then a smile drew across his lips. "Miss Lark and I have known each other quite some time," he said. "We have attended many such events during our acquaintance."

Cyril grinned, chuckling and nodding his approval. "Touché. I had quite forgotten the extent of your acquaintance. I shan't forget again, shall I? Now, back to the quadrille, Miss Lark. You will mark me on your card?"

She nodded for lack of knowledge of another response. The brothers Rexley were quite a pair, all at once seeming both at odds and in alliance with one another. She wondered what it would have been like had she had siblings of her own.

Her eyes misted over as her mind thought of the dim possibility. Had she had siblings they probably would have perished in the fire with the rest of her family.

Without asking permission, Jonathon took her hand. "Shall we have a go at this waltz?"

She smiled and silently rebuked the butterflies that fluttered inside her at the prospect. She had nothing to fear. She had danced the waltz with him many times over.

Yes, and she had crushed his toes more times than that!

"Are you all right?" Jonathon's worried voice brought her fretting mind back to itself. "You have a grip on my arm as tight as death," he observed.

Her eyes traveled to where she held his forearm as they approached the dance floor arm in arm. The vision of her stiffened grasp surprised her. She was completely unaware she had even the strength inside her to produce such a vise. She forced her grip to ease and showed him an apologetic countenance.

"Don't be afraid. I promise not to allow my pain to show. Should you step on my toes, not a soul will be the wiser." He grinned, and she knew he was teasing her.

She could not help but be infected by the gaiety. She

had crushed his feet so many times, he had most likely grown calluses of protection on them. They were laughing still when he took her in his arms and began moving her rhythmically round the dance floor.

She felt like a princess in his arms as he twirled her, his leading touch light yet strong. She ignored the stares and deliberately focused on his cravat. It was impeccably tied, impeccably white with a hint of pattern woven into the fabric so expertly that only at this close range could it be discerned. She closed her eyes and reveled in the music. Dancing with Jonathon in the quiet library had been an exercise, but waltzing with him with the music to imbibe her was an indescribable experience. She felt lighter than air as Jonathon skillfully twirled her around the floor.

Her eyes fluttered up to his face, and he smiled down at her. "You are lovely, Miss Lark, and I cannot tell you how grateful I am that the good Countess Lieven introduced this most sinful dance to us that I might hold you this closely under the scrutiny of others."

Heat rose within her like steam from a pot of boiling water. Indeed, she thought she might boil over herself. Yet, the warmth was not frightening, but ever sublime.

She didn't find the dance to be sinful, but she couldn't say the same for the corruption of her innocent thoughts. Suddenly she wished they were once again dancing in the confines of the library—not to hide from Society, but for the intimacy the room provided.

Her eyes moved from his, and she scanned the room.

They were indeed under scrutiny; all eyes seemed to be upon them. Lark realized she cared not a whittle. She smiled brightly and drank in the exaltation brought on by waltzing with Jonathon. She was accustomed to living her life in exile, why should she care if she were not accepted now? She had been silly to worry. She needed to focus only on Jonathon holding her in his arms. That was all that mattered.

And then she espied the Marchioness of Abberley. The woman leaned over and whispered something to another finely dressed lady. That lady pointed a gloved finger in Lark's direction, her mouth fallen open.

Lark strained to find them again and again as

Jonathon twirled her around the room. Dread dampened her spirits and her stomach searched for her boot buttons. All joy dissolved as quickly as it had risen. She wanted to scream at Jonathon to stop moving her; she wanted to see the women, to decipher what they were saying as they pointed at her—at *her*.

With the effect of a toppled house of cards, the news traveled down the row of ladies. As each lady turned to the next, that one cast a shocked glance in her direction, then cocked an ear to the next in line. Then, as if to add insult, when it came her turn, Lady Wescotte allowed the gossip to continue without apparent hindrance or correction.

Lark felt as if she were a moth caught within the glass encasement of a sconce. Suddenly she was center stage and trapped. Surely, like the moth, the heat would become too intense and she would perish.

She closed her eyes and tried to forget the meddlesome women. They were strangers, she told herself—well most of them. What did it matter, their opinion? Hadn't she just decided it didn't matter?

It mattered.

She was not so naïve. She knew of the ridicule Lord Peter had received. She had overheard arguments between Jonathon and his father, between Cyril and his father, over the why's of what he had done to them. She was not so naïve to think it didn't matter—she merely wished to be.

Decidedly, she trumped up some inner courage she had not known existed and opened her eyes. If they were going to criticize her for not being able to speak, she certainly was not going to give them an added reason to flap their lips. She was going to show them she knew thoroughly how to dance.

Despite her conviction, her eyes strayed once again. This time they fell not on the ladies, but on Nigel Aubury. She didn't know how her gaze had found him, he was almost completely hidden by a large potted tree. Perhaps that is what drew her attention. His intense gaze followed her across the dance floor as if she were a two-headed snake.

Like the visions of a nightmare, she could not forget

his locale. Each time she was twirled in his direction, she found him all too easily. His watery gaze filled her with anxiety his examination was so fierce. There was a feral look to him that chilled Lark through to the bone, and regardless of how she tried, she could not shake the uneasy feeling.

The stale cake she had partaken of earlier became rancid in her stomach, and her legs tried to give way. She looked with desperate eyes to Jonathon and was gratefully aware when he perceived all was not right with her.

Chapter Nineteen

"You are unwell," he said unnecessarily as he led her away from the other revelers.

I am well she wanted to scream out. But it would have been a lie, even if she had found her tongue. In truth, the rejection of the other women didn't overset her as much as Aubury's gaze. He truly looked as if he hated her—and that could not be since she did not even know the gentleman.

Jonathon led her out into the night. The evening breeze washed her with chilled air and a shiver racked her body.

"Forgive me," Jonathon said. "Stay well and I'll return presently." He left her for only a moment and returned carrying her pelisse. Wrapping it around her shoulders, he held her close to his body.

"I should hope no one sees us thus," he told her, "else both our reputations will be ruined. But I dare not let you catch your death."

Lark leaned into him, not caring about her reputation. His strong arms around her were enough to make her feel safe. She didn't want to go back inside—ever. She wanted to remain in her safe haven at Somerset Manor, with no knowledge of Society —and with Society having no knowledge of her.

She still could not comprehend why Lord Peter had thought she needed protection, and neither did she care. The *ton* was a harsh lot, and she wanted nothing further to do with them. Surely if she disappeared again, the need for protection would be ended.

A shudder overcame her again and Jonathon's grip tightened on her arm. "Do you wish to go inside? Before, you looked as if you needed some fresh air else you might swoon, but we can go back indoors if you are cold."

She shook her head. Inside was decidedly bad. She

watched a fine carriage pulled by a team of four white horses pass along the road. Even at this late hour, people were out and about, she thought. Why? she wondered. It was much more comforting to remain behind locked doors. Lord Peter may have been criticized for his reclusive behavior, but in her opinion, he had the right of it. After all her yearning to be free, Lord Peter had had the right of it. How ironic.

"Would you like to explain what overset you so?" The sound of Jonathon's voice vibrated through his chest and skittered across her back. It was odd how comforting just a sound could be.

She twisted to see his face. Worry was evident in the hard lines that now creased his brow. That was comforting, too. Whether the truth be that he thought of her merely as a responsibility or as a wife, at least she meant something to him in some small way. But how could she tell him of her terrifying experience? It was utterly indefinable. She had been afraid of a look, of a stare, of a few frustrated, haughty gossiping women.

"You must trust me, Lark. If we're to be married, you must trust me explicitly. I would never wish harm on you."

She pulled away from him, then, so she could speak, but the sudden chill stunned her to speechlessness. She had not fully realized the comfort of his warmth until the sweet contact was severed. Desolation claimed her. If she told him she was consumed by fear of just a look from a stranger, what would he think of her? Even *she* thought her reaction was irrational. Surely, a man as strong and immovable as Lord Somerset would think her childish—and a child was far from the image she wished him to embrace.

"I am fine," she signed. "I merely became too hot. So many people, you understand. I am not used to such activity. I do apologize if I caused you worry. That was not my intention. I—"

He showed her his palm. "Please, slow down."

Her hands slowed. "I am sorry. I am overly agitated this evening. I was so afraid I would bring you shame." The words had sprung from her fingers before she realized what she was saying. Embarrassed, she dropped her head, studying the crystal white gloves covering her hands.

She felt, more than heard, when he moved towards her. Her eyes moved from her fingers to the finely polished boots covering his feet.

The warmth of his hands upon her shoulders startled her. She had not imagined that he would touch her. Even through the thick pelisse and ample material of her gown's short sleeves, his heat penetrated her body. She lifted her head slowly and came to meet his gaze.

It was her undoing. Raw affection shone in the depths of his dark eyes the likes of which she had never experienced. She swallowed the lump of awareness that rose in her throat as her eyes threatened to spill with tears.

Turning her head, she avoided his eyes, but he did not allow it. Slowly he moved his hand up her arm and with a single finger, turned her face toward his once again.

"No," he said huskily. "Don't turn away." He cupped her chin in his hand, and she wondered absently how he had managed to move from her arm to her chin without ever breaking the contact between them. "Do you not know you could never bring me shame, Lark Blackwell?"

He caressed her cheek. "You are a daffodil after a spring shower. My life has been a thunderstorm—A struggle to fit into something I never actually believed worthwhile. Yet, I would not change a moment of my wait for sunshine, for you are the flower that blooms from the bud of all my discord."

A single tear spilled from her eye and she wrenched free of his tender grasp to hide her face and swipe the traitor from view.

"I'm sorry if I embarrass you," he declared. "I know I am much your senior, and you think of me in the same regard as you did my father, but I cannot help the way I feel."

He scanned her face and saw innocence and fright shining in her light eyes. A fist of pain closed around his heart. Anguish constricted his chest. He wanted so badly to take her in his arms, show her the love he felt for her.

He broke the contact between them, clenching his

fists at his side. He could touch her no longer. It was too painful, too tempting, too wrong and so right. He was a nodcock to have allowed his feelings for her to grow when it was a love forbidden.

She raised her arms into the light, but he stopped her. "Come," he said quickly, "Let us join the others." He attempted to steer her in the direction of the door, but she pulled away in protest. He turned to look at her in question.

She shook her head. "I do not wish to return," she told him silently.

"But we must. We have delayed much too long. People will talk."

"Let them." She stared at him doe-eyed, yet with a determination burning behind her innocence.

He gave a short laugh. "You are indeed unaware of the repercussions of such a decision. We must return," he urged. He took her arm and again tried to escort her inside.

She pulled away a second time. "I feel we must talk," she said when she was free of his grasp.

He looked around, checking for onlookers, but found none. "All right," he agreed slowly. Anxiety rose in his throat.

A chasm of silence separated them for several moments before she spoke. Her movements were slow and deliberate. He swallowed and consciously felt his skin move with the slide of his Adam's apple. The trepidation would not digest.

He watched her hands without blinking, without breathing, without a beat of heart.

And she surprised him.

"I...I was...afraid. I was afraid I would always be...a thorn...in your...side. An unwanted burden thrust upon you by Lord...Peter. I did not think...that...you could...*love* me as I love you. I thought..."

He read no more.

He grabbed her hands in both of his. "Say no more!" Confusion waltzed across her face and he could feel her pulse beneath his fingers. Her eyes pooled with tears, a single, salty droplet spilling over. Jonathon watched the tear make its sad descent down her ivory cheek, and his

147

heart collapsed. He gently squeezed her hands, trying desperately to find words of comfort. None came.

She wrenched free of his grasp.

"Why do I sicken you so," she signed. "One moment it is as if you care for me, the next it is as if you loathe the very sight of me. I am at a loss."

He heaved in a breath. "Because, my dear, you may very well be my sister."

In one quick, fluid motion, Lark stepped up and struck him in the face.

Chapter Twenty

Lark was in full nightdress when Rebekka sat her down that evening. "Do you know why Lord Peter kept you hidden all these years? Why you must assume a false sir name until the wedding vows are spoken?"

Lark did not know until this very moment that she could feel any worse. "No, why? Do you?" she signed slowly.

Rebekka shook her head. "I do not know exactly. I am but a servant. It was never my place to question. I knew Lord Peter must have ample reason. He wanted to protect you. I wanted to protect you, also. You were but a child."

Lark's impatience heightened. "Be direct," she signed, her disquiet showing in the trembling of her fingers.

"Did you not recognize any of the members present this evening?"

Lark sighed. "I have seen no one save the Rexley members at Lord Peter's will reading for more than a decade gone. Who do you suppose I should have been able to recognize? And why, praytell am I to be protected?"

"I didn't think of it until this very night, and still I do not have proof for you to purchase..." she paused and Lark filled in the silence with an impatient groan.

Rebekka continued. "Blackwell House has been rebuilt. I have known this fact for some time. There is talk even among servants."

"How can this be? There are but two who survived of that house and we are both in this very room." Lark lowered her hands to her lap and watched an array of emotions play on her abigail's face. An uneasy feeling washed over her. She grew very still.

"You have a cousin, my lady. That man inherited the estate when you were presumed to have perished with your parents. The eldest of your Aunt Beril's son."

At the name, Lark vaguely remembered Aunt Beril. She was a stately woman who had married a Scotsman—someone of a lower rank.

She turned to Rebekka. "Why was I not sent to live with Aunt Beril?" She signed slowly, not at all sure she actually wanted to hear the answer.

Rebekka shrugged. "I cannot presume to understand. Perhaps Lord Peter thought it best if you remained dead as everyone thought you were. I have my own doubts as to how good a parent your aunt was." She darted apologetic eyes to Lark. "I am sorry, miss. I spoke out of turn."

Lark shrugged off the insult to her kin. "Tell me why you say this?"

"Her sons, my lady. Neither was of a good seed." Rebekka turned her eyes to the floor momentarily then looked up again, a new thought shining in her eyes. "It was a good thing you were not sent to her anyway. Your Aunt Beril got the consumption not long after the fire and was bedridden the rest of her days."

Lark digested Rebekka's words about as easily as she had swallowed the stale cakes at Almack's. She was disturbed by the confession. Confused. Absolutely stunned. She had kin. She had kin who had lived—and died—without her knowledge. Until this moment, she had not realized just how isolated she had truly been.

She slapped her hand on the hand-sewn quilt to get Rebekka's attention. "This cousin, he is the one who rebuilt Blackwell House?"

Rebekka nodded.

"Why did you not tell me? He is family. He cannot be so completely bad, and I should have liked to visit it."

"Lord Peter instructed me to keep my mouth and my mind at bay."

"But why?"

Rebekka shrugged. "I don't know, I do but what I'm told." She peered into Lark's eyes as if trying to see into her soul. "You recognized no one?"

"I have already told you." She looked pointedly at Rebekka. "Now, you tell me."

Rebekka fidgeted in the gilt chair. "Nigel Aubury—"

Lark's blood turned to ice, and she chilled all over.

She raised a hand to silence her maid. "Do not mention that man to me. He is...frightening. He stared maliciously at me all eve, and I could have sworn he even followed Lord Somerset and me out of doors!"

"He is the youngest of your cousins," Rebekka confessed quietly.

"Lies." Lark signed the single word with such vehemence in her motion that it screamed across the distance between them. "He is..."

"This is my deduction as to Lord Peter keeping you to himself. Your Aunt Beril was lacking in her motherly duties. Your father was Lord Peter's bosom friend. He did not want his friend's only daughter raised by such personages."

"But you don't know this for certain? There could be no other reason?"

"That is why I have never voiced such opinions in the past. They are but speculation on a lowly servant's part. But when *he* approached and I took to recognizing him, I thought it high time I told you."

"High time, indeed. Speculation or none, you should have told me before this day."

Lark's rebuke sailed past its mark. Rebekka shrugged. "You were but a child. In my eye you are still but a child."

"Seventeen," Lark protested silently. She lowered her hands and clutched the quilt to her breast, deep in thought. For several moments neither woman moved. Then Lark released her so her grip could speak. "This still does not explain why I am to be protected. Why I am to relinquish my family name."

"I have no answer to that. I have but always listened to Lord Peter's instruction knowing full well that he had your interests in mind."

"That is not a very good answer," Lark bemoaned with quick fingers and a down-turned mouth. "What of Jonathon?"

"What of Lord Somerset?" Rebekka replied.

Nicola Beaumont

Chapter Twenty-One

Lark spent a restless night, her thoughts spinning with the details of Rebekka's conjecture and Lord Somerset's shocking remarks regarding her parentage. She was in high dudgeon this new morn and did not look forward to spending the day on a scheduled outing with her betrothed.

She shed her morning frock for an empire dress of an emerald hue. The mantuamaker had convinced Lark that the dress would do her up proud and the seamstress had not been mistaken. The high waistline accented her bosoms in a way that suddenly pleased her. At least she would look all-the-thing, even if she did not feel so inside.

Rebekka skillfully piled layers of pale blonde hair so that silken ringlets cascaded down to her shoulder blades. Lark was pleased with the reflection she projected from the looking glass as Rebekka topped her hair with a delectable bonnet trimmed with white lace and green ribbon.

As Lark descended the stairs, Jonathon waited at the bottom. Her heart collapsed. It was difficult to remain angry with him when just the site of him stirred her so, but the apprehension and hurt still lingered and she could not forget his insult. She twitched a tentative smile.

"I thought I was going to have to come above and drag you down," he said when she appeared on the landing.

She didn't reply for fear of letting go of the banister.

"The day grows old," he told her, "but you are as fresh as Spring."

She reached the bottom of the staircase, and he took her hand, holding her at arms length while he inspected the dress that was new to him. "That color suits you well, my dear."

She gently pulled her hand away from his. "How can

152

you be so civil after insulting my mother and Lord Peter thus, last eve?

Jonathon took up both of her hands. "We will speak of this presently—when we are privately together on our outing. I would not for the world, bring you distress."

"Rebekka will be down presently," she signed, ignoring his remarks. She didn't know what to make of them, anyway. If he hadn't wanted to bring her distress, why had he accused her mother and his father of such debauchery? Why had he insinuated she was illegitimate?

He helped her into her mantle and then donned a top hat and overcoat himself. He made a handsome figure. She loved him more than she wanted to; perhaps that were why his accusation lacerated her heart.

"What is running through that head of yours?"

She shook her head in reply. How could she tell him he had wounded her? How could she tell him it was beyond comprehension for them to be siblings? How could she tell him it would kill her if it were true?

Rebekka arrived and they were just to leave when the doorknocker sounded. Chauncy came from within the kitchen, but Jonathon waved him away. "We are about to take our leave. I shall see to the door."

Chauncy disappeared silently.

Jonathon opened the door and the young messenger \standing out of doors quickly snatched the cap from his head. "I 'ave a missive 'ere for Jonafin Rexley, Lawd Sumaset."

"Yes, I am he." He took the note from the boy's extended hand and broke the seal. The boy had turned to leave when Jonathon stopped him. "Wait one moment. I must reply." He turned to the women. "I apologize for the delay. This is quite important business." He disappeared inside, leaving them standing in the vestibule.

He disappeared into his study for just a moment then returned posthaste and handed a message to the errand boy along with a shiny shilling.

The boy beamed. "Fank ya, Guvna," he repeated more than once before he scurried along at not a slow pace.

****

Hyde Park entertained a throng of carriages and fine

horseflesh. Rebekka and Jonathon had both attempted to describe the bustle of an afternoon ride in Hyde Park, but after seeing it for herself, Lark realized their second-hand descriptions did not do justice to the clamoring liveliness.

The array of colors worn by the ladies, most of whom had plumes atop their heads, had the place looking more like a painting than an out-of-doors park. Horses' hooves pounded the ground, the staccato sound forming an unbidden melody in Lark's ear.

Despite wanting to remain aloof, she had a newfound personal confidence as she sat beside Jonathon in his fine carriage drinking in all the stares of couples they passed along the way. She noticed many lean to their partners, but she did not mind the gossip today.

"You attract much attention," Jonathon told her.

She looked at him most boldly and smiled. "The attention is not as dreadful as I had first anticipated," she told him honestly, grateful for once for her ability to converse without worry of someone overhearing.

Jonathon's eyebrows rose. "My, you've mustered some confidence, haven't you? I must say, it's most becoming on you."

Lark's traitorous skin turned pink.

"Ah, but still an innocent," Jonathon observed. "And that becomes you just as much."

"You are incorrigible," Lark told him. "If I were a speaking lady, you would not address me in such a forward manner."

"Wouldn't I? I daresay it has nothing to do with your ability to speak. I have quite mastered your language well enough, I should say."

"What, then? Is it more then that you think I am your sister?" Lark grunted and turned her face away from him.

Jonathon sighed. Her words pierced him, but he deserved no less. He should have held his emotions and kept his mouth closed, but his brain had turned to gruel as she had spoken of love. How much more difficult would it be to hold her at a distance, knowing she returned his feelings?

A carriage pulled up beside them and the gentleman doffed his hat. Lark smiled, and the lady seated beside him looked thoroughly overset. She picked up the closed parasol at her side and slammed it against the carriage floor in the most ungenteel way.

The man's head snapped away from Jonathon and Lark, his full attention now on the one he had chosen to escort.

Jonathon laughed and waved as his friend nervously glanced their way. "Winston is up to his tricks again," he said to himself as he watched them pull away.

Lark patted his arm and his attention returned to her. "You are attempting to avoid the subject," she told him.

He showed her a blank look. "Subject?"

"Of why you can conceive we are siblings, yet still maintain this charade of a betrothal. You think that Lord Peter wished to wed brother to sister? 'Tis utmost disgusting."

Jonathon sighed. "I cannot tell you all, but I can reason no other explanation for my father ordering me to protect you. And under circumstances of which I am unable to disclose, it is perfectly natural for me to conclude the sibling relation. After all, you are hid away and kept in my father's house—he obviously cared for you as a father does his child; You share his birth blemish on your arm, and I am distinctly aware at times how your mouth tilts into a smile much the way did his."

Lark didn't know how to respond. She sat beside him in disbelief. He had to have lost his mind to make so weighty a conclusion based on such feathery evidence. She raised her hands to say as much but he didn't give her the chance to speak.

"I didn't wish to burden you with such information until I became more certain, but you seemed so overset by my reluctance to...to...well, perhaps we should seek a less nocuous subject of conversation." He glanced to Rebekka.

"I haven't had much experience with the world, yet even I realize that when people live with one another they develop like characteristics. Mayhap I smile in a similar manner as Lord Peter, but it means nothing. I fear I also have Rebekka's disposition. Would you conclude that she were my mother?"

Jonathon waved away her statement. "And the

blemish on your arm?"

"I fear you are shameful," Lark told him finally.

"I'm sorry, I didn't catch the first part," he said.

"She said you are shameful," Rebekka cut in from her place aside. "And I should agree."

Jonathon gave Rebekka a surprised look then glanced at Lark. Laughter bubbled inside Lark's throat until she could contain it no longer. The notion was just so preposterous.

The sound of Lark's laughter doused Jonathon like a bucket of cold water on a hot, muggy day—at once startling, but not at all unpleasant. Even an operatic diva had never produced so lovely a melody as that which rang in his ears this very first time he experienced Lark's laughter. His breath caught in his chest.

He grieved anew for the loss of being able to hear spoken words come from her tender mouth—all those beautiful sounds he would never hear her utter.

He swallowed his breath and looked into her face, studying her every feature. He wondered what was dancing around in her pretty head.

At that moment, a baroque pulled up to engage them in conversation. Lark looked over to find Nigel Aubury smiling back. Her body chilled. She forced her tightened lips into some semblance of a smile in return, although, it took all her will to accomplish it.

"Good afternoon to you," Aubury said.

Jonathon acknowledged him with a nod.

"Tatt's later?"

Lark's body grew more rigid as she realized Aubury was going to lengthen the conversation. She turned her face away from him and toward Jonathon. He did not seem to notice her anxiety, for he merely gave her a faint smile, answered Aubury's question, and posed one of his own.

She fixed her gaze on the hem of her dress. She could see the tips of her boots poking out.

"Have you seen Wessex's stallion? I have heard stories of its stature."

"'Tis a magnificent specimen for certain," Aubury replied. "And are you quite the thing this morning, Miss Black—Blackburn?"

Lark's gaze bolted to his face. He smiled but it did nothing to better his looks. Just then, he began to sneeze and quickly pulled a handkerchief from his pocket.

"Excuse me," he apologized. "Observed you looked a little underdone last evening," he continued. "Rotten case of megrims or some such female ailment? You are better, I hope."

She looked to Jonathon a second time, pleading with her eyes for him to rescue her from this turmoil. His perception was rightly targeted this time as a troubled look found a home on his face.

"She is well," he answered for her, and relief enveloped her.

"Ah, that is good."

Jonathon seemed suddenly in a hurry to depart. "We must be on our way, Aubury. I shall see you at Tatt's next time I am able to attend." He snapped the reins before Aubury had time to say anything more.

Lark's entire body relaxed the moment the horses hooves clipped the street.

"There is something the matter," he said.

She shook her head.

"Do not begin with this again," he told her bristly. "I was positive we were past coy games of mistrust. If there is something the matter, you will tell me this instant. I insist."

She looked at him reservedly but bolstered courage when he returned her gaze with one of comfort. "Do you think he is your relation, too?" she signed in clipped movements.

Chapter Twenty-Two

Jonathon scanned the room as he waited for Drew
Hollingsworth. Watier's was a bustle of activity, and
Jonathon feared their conversation would be overheard.
Hollingsworth's missive had not indicated the nature of
his uncoverings, but if it fared disparaging to Lark's
parentage, Jonathon certainly did not want anyone to
overhear of it.

He disposed of his meal sparingly, picking at the
Shepherd's pie with little enthusiasm. Apprehension
mixed with the meal in his stomach as he impatiently
waited for his friend's arrival. It was a far from pleasant
feeling.

He sipped on his brandy. The copper liquid burned
his throat and warmed his stomach. Despite the throng of
gentlemen, Jonathon felt an unsettling chill and the
brandy served as a welcome respite.

He smiled tightly at a gentleman passing his corner
table then returned his attention to the door. If
Hollingsworth did not arrive post haste Jonathon feared
he would choke on the trepidation his throat refused to
swallow.

When Hollingsworth came through the door,
Jonathon was not appeased, however. Instead, he found
the tension in his throat grew to the expanse of his entire
body. Even his toes tingled with all the alert and dreadful
possibilities he had but contemplated.

Hollingsworth smiled as he came to the table. He
leaned his cane against the table's edge and took his seat.
"You look in queer stirrups, my friend," he observed
casually.

"Let's be done with this," Jonathon hissed, scanning
the room once again for eavesdroppers.

Hollingsworth seemed unmoved. "Remember, it was
you who commissioned me to this investigation."

"You state the obvious. Get on with it." Jonathon swilled the brandy in his glass, took a healthy drink then fixed his eyes on his friend once again.

"I don't care for a drink," Hollingsworth said sarcastically. At Jonathon's warning glare, Hollingsworth put up a conciliatory palm. "All right." From memory, he relayed what he had discovered.

"There really didn't seem much to uncover. The fire was considered an accident, as you know. There was never any suspicion of foul play. I realized this would not satisfy, mind you, so I investigated further. It was quite a nuisance at the onset, I can tell you."

Jonathon's patience was threadbare. "I apologize for the inconvenience. Get to the point."

"Tut, tut," Hollingsworth chided. "As I investigated further some interesting facts arose." He paused, obviously for effect and Jonathon silently cursed the day his friend was born. "Were you of the knowledge that Nigel Aubury was not the initial heir to the Blackwell property?"

Jonathon shook his head. "I did not keep up with such triviality. Truthfully, once my mother was gone and Father put us out, I didn't think much of the Blackwells at all."

"Mmm. Well, Putnam, Nigel's older brother was the first to come by the estate. In fact, he took residence of the place as soon as Fire Protection had sufficiently rebuilt the House."

Jonathon forced himself to remember twelve years past. He studied the air but could not recall Putnam ever residing at Blackwell House. "I thought Putnam kicked up his boot heels not long after the fire."

Hollingsworth nodded and adjusted in the chair. "Yes," he said, awe reverberating in his tone. "But that is not the crux of it. Putnam died under very mysterious circumstances."

Jonathon wished he had paid more attention to what had happened all that time ago. But he had been so sick with grief over the loss of his mother that he had scarcely cared for his own life during those early months following the tragedy. "Was he not struck by an accident?"

"Horse kicked him in the head somehow. Events are

159

still unclear as there were no actual witnesses. But—and here is the most interesting of things—it was suspected that Nigel had something to do with it." He rested back in his chair, a satisfied grin on his face.

"I cannot believe such things. If that were the case, why was there no investigation?"

"Ah, well, 'twas all speculation, you see. You would not believe the low places I had to go to retrieve this information."

"I have heard plenty about your escapades, old chap," Jonathon replied, not wanting to know first-hand the lengths his friend went to gather piquant information. "But speculation does me no good. I need to know of the danger to Miss Lark. What of—"

A waiter came and asked if they needed refreshments, and Jonathon impatiently told him not to return.

Hollingsworth turned surprised eyes to his friend. "Brutal. It was not him that did it, you know."

"Tell me more of Nigel Aubury," Jonathon had never been fond of Aubury, and Lark had obviously taken an immediate dislike to him. Perhaps there really was something sinister there.

Hollingsworth shrugged. "That is really all there is to tell. But we all know what a greedy hugger-mugger he is. All seems perfectly logical to me. He did in his own brother for the inheritance of Blackwell House. It is a rather substantial estate."

"Shh!" Jonathon looked about. "You cannot make such accusations without proof. Aubury would have your head. Besides, what of Lark? None of this reveals why my father would think she needed protection."

Hollingsworth's mouth dropped open. "Are you daft? It is the most perfect conclusion of all." Hollingsworth shook his head in disgust. "You used to be awake on every suit. Has this woman addled your brain? If she were to be found alive, she would be able to claim her rightful inheritance, even though she is merely a woman."

Jonathon shook his head. "*Now*, yes. But what of twelve years ago? Neither Aubury, nor his brother, would have ever received the property had my father allowed Lark's survival to be known. Nigel would have felt no threat, would have had nothing to hide...Unless..." He thought for a moment. His father's letter had revealed the fire was not really an accident. "Unless—"

"Unless, Aubury had set the fire himself," Hollingsworth finished impatiently.

"There is just one thing wrong with this theory," Jonathon went on.

"And what is that? I need a drink now." Hollingsworth hailed a waiter. The young man approached them quite warily. "See what you have done," Hollingsworth told Jonathon. "You have shattered the poor chap's confidence. He shall never be the same again."

Jonathon ignored the comment, although he did observe the waiter suddenly recoil.

Hollingsworth ordered a brandy for himself and another for Jonathon then returned to the subject at hand. "And what is that?" he repeated.

"Nigel was not the first to claim ownership. Why would he have set the fire in order for his older brother to receive the estate? Doesn't make sense."

Hollingsworth refused to meet Jonathon's gaze and Jonathon knew his friend well enough to realize not all was set to light.

"Out with it," Jonathon said and, when Hollingsworth shot him a questioning glance, explained, "You have a very expressive face. Tell me."

"It is merely that although you cannot seem to attend the idea, it is quite clear to me. It is well known that both the Aubury men were, shall we say, *different.* It is not past my inclination to believe that perhaps the older Aubury committed the fire and Nigel in turn did him in later."

The waiter brought the drinks and scurried away without delay. Jonathon took a sip. "That is possible, I suppose."

"Highly possible," Hollingsworth urged, much too vehemently for Jonathon's liking.

"There is something you're not telling me." Jonathon felt that rise of anxiety swell within him. He had known Hollingsworth a long time and something was definitely amiss.

"It is nothing I can tell you until I have further

161

investigated."

"Tell me regardless."

"I shan't. It is of no consequence as yet."

"You shall, or I shall make known of your escapades in Surrey."

"You wouldn't dare."

"Perhaps not. But are you willing to take a chance? You live on the fringes of society as it is."

Hollingsworth leaned forward, placing his brandy on the table between them. "I know you are bluffing. We have had a go at cards one too many times. I know your game."

Jonathon sighed. "All right. So I will not spoil your reputation, such as it is. But please, I am weary. Just tell me what you know. I understand it is speculation and shall take it as such."

Hollingsworth took in a considerable breath. "Aubury...well, Aubury acquired the estate from the actual heir. According to the fire protection and the will of Miss Lark's father, there was an underlying stipulation that if Miss Lark, or any future heirs born after her, were to perish before Blackwell's own death...Peter Rexley would become sole owner of Blackwell House." He let out his breath and sat mutely while Jonathon drank in the information.

The silence stretched between them and Hollingsworth began to fidget. Jonathon stared at him blankly. He felt as if he had just been shot in the chest by a dueling pistol.

Finally, he found his tongue. "I do not understand. If my father was heir, then why did he not merely allow Lark's survival to be known? Wouldn't the fire have been an accident in that case?"

"I have posed the same questions to myself more than once. My explanation is quite plausible. You see, Aubury would naturally assume himself as heir. As Lark's cousin, it would be highly unusual for Blackwell to bequeath his holdings to a member outside the family."

Jonathon nodded.

"He sets the fire thinking to gain for himself and is disappointed afterward when he discovers the truth."

"Go on," Jonathon prompted.

"Your father somehow discovers the deed. I do not know how, but it is possible. When he confronts Aubury, Aubury threatens to kill him also if he doesn't hand over the property to him as the rightful family heir. Of course, your father, being the upright gentleman that he was would see the immediate danger in allowing Lark's survival to become known and does as Aubury wishes in order to save Lark's life."

"'Tis true my father would not have needed, nor wanted, I suspect, Blackwell House. He had his own estate to contend with." Jonathon thought further. "Yes, that would possibly explain why he would feel the ongoing need to protect Lark, but if he knew of the fire being set by Aubury, why did he not just call in the Robin Redbreasts."

"That I don't understand, unless Aubury threatened your father with something else."

"Damnation!" Jonathon hissed across the table. "Why couldn't my father just have explained everything? This is most vexing."

"Indeed. Nevertheless, you must agree that we have uncovered a very good reason for Lark to need protection, and is that not what you were after? I should be wary of Nigel Aubury, if I were you. No matter what happened twelve years ago, he is the one who will lose all should Lark's identity be revealed."

"You have the truth of it," Jonathon replied. He leaned forward. "A word in your ear." He waited for Hollingsworth to close the gap across the table. "What of Miss Lark's parentage? Did you uncover any information regarding that?"

Chapter Twenty-Three

"Have you not before tried to speak?"

Lark shot a nervous look across the picnic blanket to Jonathon. The bite of chicken lodged in her throat forcing her to swallow hard several times to coax it down.

He had to ruin it.

He had surprised her with this wonderful luncheon, just the two of them on his property surrounded by blossoming trees, a soft, cooling breeze and the most delectable meal. And now he had to broach the subject of speech.

She had thought of that a great deal lately, but fear had overcome her at every instant. She couldn't speak to him, no matter how much they both wished it.

She put the chicken leg on the plate and wiped her hands with a napkin before answering him. "Do you not think that were I able to speak, I would do so?"

"I'm not sure. Perhaps it's easier for you to remain silent."

"Silent and shameful rather than vocal and accepted?"

"Why did my father bring you here?" Accusation laced his tone.

Lark sat rigid, conscious of the swell and fall of her breasts as she breathed. The gusty breeze that fanned the air chilled her as much as his words.

"I have already told you. I don't know why. Nor would I purposely wed my own brother! Why don't you believe me?"

"I believe you."

"You don't sound as if you believe me. You say the words, but they are tinged with doubt."

"Do you not remember anything of the fire?"

"I remember nothing, nothing, I tell you." Her hands clipped the air as her frustration piqued. "Did you bring me out here and arrange this wonderful day merely to interrogate me?"

"Repeat that?"

Lark slapped the ground at her sides. Tears of frustration pricked the backs of her eyes. She hated that he could not always understand her. She knew she must make her movements more pronounced, but whenever emotion rose in her, she didn't feel in control of her own hands. They flew about with a will of their own. A thought entered her mind, and then was immediately produced on her hands.

She successfully fought back the tears and repeated her question.

Jonathon's will was punctured. He looked into her glossy eyes, and remorse overcame him. "No," he said quietly. "I brought you out here that we might enjoy the time together. You see, tomorrow I must take my leave for a little while."

"Because of me?"

"No, no, dear." He gave her a reassuring smile but the grim insecurity within her eyes did not fade.

"When I returned last evening there was word of some business I must attend to in Scotland. I shall only be gone a few days time, but..." His words trailed off. How could he tell her of what Hollingsworth had said? He could not, but it was imperative that she take care to remain safe while he was gone. Once he checked into some facts on Aubury's family, he might rest more easily, but not until then. "I wish for you to remain safe while I am gone. Take care when you are about. All the better, do not leave Somerset Manor while I am absent." His tone remained matter-of-fact, but inside a knot of misgiving lodged in his stomach.

"I do not understand this," she signed, thoroughly overset. "I have lived a prisoner's life all these years and now when it is unnecessary, you still wish for me to remain hidden away. I had believed all that was past."

"It won't be for much longer. I swear it. But you must obey my wishes."

"If I am in so grave a danger, why leave me at all? What were I to greet death during your absence?" Her pout punctuated her point, and Jonathon felt like an ogre.

165

For a moment, he could not respond, his sight remaining transfixed on the cloth-covered distance between them. He raised his eyes and looked into her face. "This endeavor is something I must undertake to insure your safety and that of our future. You may not understand, but if I do not see to matters now, the opportunity may not present itself again." He looked away trying to figure out a way to make her understand.

He turned his attention once again to Lark. "No one knows of your residence here. If you stay on the estate, I am confident you will be safe."

Lark expelled a breath laden with frustration. "I am a child no longer. Tell me why Lord Peter thought to protect me. Tell me why you order me imprisoned. Perhaps if I know the danger, I will share your belief in a need for caution." Her arms seemed limp and weary as she spoke, and Jonathon wished he could tell her more.

"If I knew exactly, I would tell you. However, my father saw fit to keep it undisclosed. He kept a great many secrets, I am beginning to discover..."

Jonathon's voice trailed off and a degree of sadness found its way into his eyes.

Lark took pity on him. She had lived her entire life on this estate—and would likely live the rest of it here as Lady Somerset. Not long past, she had hoped to lock herself away forever and never have to face another soul again. Ironic that a mere trice later, she would have such a change of heart that she now sat here fighting for her freedom.

"All right," she signed, but he was not looking at her. She leaned over, closing the distance between them, and touched his arm. His head darted upward, and he searched her face. "All right," she began again. "I will honor your wishes and remain on the estate until your return. But there is one stipulation."

"What is that?"

"That when you can explain all of this, you will do so in detail. It is not fair that I should not know why I have lived the life I have."

Jonathon nodded. "Done."

****

"I am going to miss morning tea out here with you,"

Jonathon said two days later.

Lark turned worried eyes to him. "But you said you would only be away for a few days."

He smiled. "That I will, but I have become entirely too accustomed to seeing your beautiful face every morning. I shall become a withered man without you."

"You flatter me excessively," Lark signed. "But I shall miss you, also. These past days have been quite tolerable."

Jonathon laughed. "I know I have been a bit of a cad. But, was I so bad you deem 'tolerable' a realized goal?"

"I merely mean to say you have not treated me so much like a sister as a companion."

"I shall be honest with you. It is my very hope you are not my kin, dear Miss Lark. I quite hold you in high regard and do not wish for a...*platonic* marriage."

"You are reprehensible, my lord! To say such things to a lady." She pouted sufficiently to show her disapproval then smiled at him, unable to maintain the façade.

"Your lips are so sweet. I am sure a sound uttered from them would be just as sweet. I do wish you could speak."

Her smile faded. "I doubt I will ever be able to speak to you. Do not wish it so. I can't bear the burden of knowing you are so disappointed in me." She studied her hands, avoiding his eyes completely.

Silence descended upon them. Only the hint of a breeze and the occasional chirp of a sparrow breached the gazebo. Jonathon leaned over and took her hand, encapsulating it with both of his. "Remove the worry from your countenance. If you never utter a word, I shall marry you still. I merely mention it because I remember your impertinence as a child. You had no trouble voicing your opinion then."

She looked at him, her vision clouded by pools of unshed tears.

"Please do not cry. I am ever so sorry. I shan't mention it again," he said at once.

The dam broke and tears streamed down her face. He reached under her bonnet and wiped them dry with the pad of his thumb. "I have stolen your journal writing time this morning, haven't I? I wish to spend as much time with you as possible before I am forced to take my leave." He nudged her chin up with the side of his hand. "Lark, please do not cry; it tears my heart."

She stared. The tears had stopped but her sorrow inwardly endured. She wished to speak to him so much the ache of it seemed almost fatal.

Perhaps one day she would.

Chapter Twenty-Four

It rained for a week. Lark's despondency grew with each raindrop that soaked the ground. She had never before known the expanse of the manor, but now she roamed the halls freely, no one to hide from, no one to speak to. Jonathon was not due to return for ages, and Lark was not sure she would survive the time without him.

Chauncy and Penelope were the utmost best, but she could not find the will to return their hospitality. Rebekka attempted to engage her in activities several times, but Lark did not have the heart to accomplish the goal. She had given her heart to Jonathon and he had truly taken it with him when he left.

Cyril paid her a visit, saying he did not wish her to be lonely during Jonathon's absence, but she sensed he was truly there to confirm her safety. This annoyed her, and she had demanded he take his leave.

To her chagrin, Rebekka had seen fit to tone down her request during the translation and Cyril had stayed on much longer than Lark bided him welcome.

How she wished to scream to the world that she was capable of taking care of herself. And had she a voice, she would have done so without one drop of remorse.

Evening fell and the sun burst through the clouds with a red glow that proved hopeful. "Red sky at night, shepherd's delight," Rebekka told Lark as she unfastened the buttons of her gown.

"Fishwives!" Lark replied with vehement fingers.

"Beg pardon, Miss?"

"Fishwives tales. The sunset has absolutely nothing to do with the weather."

"Your lord will return shortly. 'Tis no reason to take your grief out on others. We have looked after you rightly and you treat us like servants," Rebekka replied indignantly.

"You are servants," Lark replied with rigid fingers.

"You used to be a sweet girl. Now look at you."

Lark flopped onto the bed and turned a sour look on Rebekka. "I used to think I liked being locked in this house. I used to be a child."

"The manners you show me now, you are still a child," Rebekka said without any sign of apology forthcoming. "Know your place. Lord Somerset is your fiancé. You must do what he says without question. He knows a great deal more than you."

Lark glared at Rebekka then shimmied down further into the bed. She flipped herself onto her side with a force that caused the entire bed to groan and creak in protest then closed her eyes and willed herself to sleep.

****

So what if the morning broke with the sun showing a wondrous array of spiraling rainbows on the windowpane? It had nothing to do with Rebekka's mindless superstition. Lark readied for the day without a word to Rebekka, purposefully wearing a frown that belied the secret optimism she held for the day. Today she was going to live for herself.

Morning tea on the gazebo had become her ritual over the years, but she had fast become accustomed to Jonathon's company and thus mornings now proved sadly lacking. Nevertheless, when Chauncy came with the tray, Lark tried to appear eager. She smiled at him just so.

"Morning, Miss," he said.

She nodded her reply and he quickly set down the tray and left her as he did each morning.

When Chauncey was out of sight, Lark left the gazebo, circumventing the house. With stealth, she tiptoed past the kitchen window, ducking low to keep her head from being seen through the pane. As she rounded the corner, she collided with none other than Cyril Rexley.

He reached out to steady her. "Going somewhere?"

She nodded and attempted to pass him.

"I rather think you should turn your pretty self around this instant."

Irritation rolled like dice in her stomach. She shook

her head and tried to pass him again.

"No," he said firmly.

"Yes!" she signed, knowing he could not understand. She sighed heavily and tried to make him see her point. She pounded her chest with an open palm.

"You..." he interpreted.

She nodded and smiled then turned her fingers toward the ground and wiggled her index and middle fingers to and fro.

"Walk. You walk?" He grinned. "By Jove! This is quite entertaining."

She glared at him askance then continued. She pointed to Cyril.

"Me."

She grinned, then with all her might, pushed him with both palms flat against the breast of his overcoat.

He laughed heartily. "You walk, me shove off!"

She shouldered past him and continued on her way.

"Hang on a minute." He caught up with her. "I cannot allow you to go alone, you know. Jon would have my head."

She continued to walk. "Wait. Wait! Allow me to fetch my carriage and I shall take you where you will, but you must take an oath to stay with me."

She gave in with a nod. At least she would get to leave the property, even if it were with a chaperone.

After much squabbling about leaving her unattended, Cyril relented and returned presently with a nice baroque. He helped her into the seat, then boarded the carriage himself and snapped the reins.

He turned to her. "So where are we off to?"

She shrugged.

"Hyde Park?" He suggested. "If you would like to take a walk about that is quite a pleasant place to do so."

She smiled and nodded and enjoyed the gentle breeze fanning her face.

Hyde Park awaited them virtually empty, the day too new to attract most. Thoroughly content, Lark took in the air with Cyril at her side, the silence between them not the least bit uncomfortable. She glanced up at Cyril, and he smiled at her.

"Lovely day, isn't it?"

She smiled an answer.

"It is much more agreeable with company than without, wouldn't you say?"

Lark gave him a little laugh and a shy nod in answer. This was more enjoyable than skulking about Somerset Manor.

They had not gone quite one quarter's distance of the park when two young lads scurried over to them, addressing Cyril.

"Aye, guv', vere's a gent needs a word in your ear," the taller of the two said.

"Where?" Cyril looked about. "I see no one."

"Over there." The boy pointed noncommittally. "'E gave me 'alf crown to take you."

"Can you not see I am quite preoccupied at the moment?"

"I can look after the lady, guv'," the shorter of the lads said, his chest puffed out in a show of manliness.

"'E said to mention sumfin 'bout a trip to Scotland and a couple'a gents by name of Aubury," the other boy coaxed.

At that, Lark's blood ran cold and it did not escape her notice that Cyril seemed more alert.

"The outspoken boy urged, "Said 'e's got pert'nent infamation 'bout. . . 'bout. Aw, I ain't rightly rememberin' but give us a break, guv, would ya? 'E's gunna make us give 'im back 'is money if we dan' git ya."

Cyril turned to Lark and took up her hand. "Will you be all right with the lad? I fear if I do not attend this man, Jonathon will take me to task. This information may be of grave import."

Reluctantly, Lark nodded then turned worried eyes to the shorter boy as Cyril was led away. She stepped down to stroll about.

Cyril had gone not much farther than a stone's throw when Lark heard horse's hooves pounding the ground. She spun around to see a phaeton that looked as if it had seen better days coming straight towards her. If she did not move, it would intercept and run her down, she was sure. Fear bubbled within her chest, froze her to the spot. The youngster beside her yelled, tried to pull her out of the way, then tumbled and rolled himself to safety.

Inside, her mind screamed for her to move out of the way, but her legs would not heed the warning.

Closer and closer it came. She could see the flared nostrils of the horse, hear the rickety wheels abusing the ground. Cyril's voice split the air as he yelled her name.

She opened her mouth to scream but no sound came out. Her arms rose and crossed over her face in protection, and then the world went black.

She awoke to the jostling of the phaeton rolling over the jutted road at breakneck speed. The vehicle took flight as it hit another rut. As the wheels kissed the earth once more, she felt the punishment ricochet through her body. Her aching head rattled like a baby's toy.

It was only when she tried to lift her hand to her head to quell the awful ringing, that she realized her wrists were bound.

Fear gripped her like the hand of death. She focused on the driver not really wanting to know who had done this to her.

Nigel Aubury.

If she thought she was frightened before, a new sense of dread swept over her.

She squirmed in the seat, and he turned his face on her. "Be still!" He bit out the order as if he were talking to an animal. His eyes were full of hatred, and she knew immediately that there would be no reasoning with him for her safe return to Somerset Manor.

She would have to wait it out until he decided to show his hand and reveal why he had seen fit to run her down and abduct her so unscrupulously.

And then she caught a glimpse of it: Blackwell House. The spires rose into the sky on either end of the house, presenting a majestic figure. She had not known she even held the memory of this house. In all her years, she had never been able to conjure the image of her family's home, but now it was as if she had never been gone.

Aubury slowed the carriage not at all, as they clamored over the cobblestones to the house. He dropped the reins almost before the carriage came to a complete stop and jumped down.

The sound of his boots upon the stones echoed in

Lark's head like the tolling of a bell. She urged herself to remain calm. It was the most difficult task she had ever undertaken.

He grabbed her bound wrists and yanked her out of the phaeton. She fell into his chest, and he roughly pushed her away. The underarm of her dress tore and gave way, and the cold air chilled her bared skin.

"Be careful and make haste," he told her harshly.

He thrust Lark through the front door almost before he had the portal open, and then pushed her into the vestibule without regard for her difficulty. The throbbing in her head intensified and she thought her skull might actually cave in. She closed her eyes and said a silent prayer for her safety. *Why had she not listened to Jonathon?*

"Come along." He grabbed her elbow and hauled her up the stairs. The rope binding her wrists began to cut into her skin even through the fabric of her gloves. She winced but refused to cry, for fear he would enjoy the knowledge of her pain.

Through her panicky misgivings came the desire to roam her home once again. He had shoved her so quickly through the ground floor and up the stairs that she had barely had time to think about her steps let alone drink in the house she had once called home. The last time she had seen it, it had been an inferno, yet here it stood, exacting memories for her.

He threw open a door almost to the end of the first floor corridor and pushed her inside. She stumbled over her skirt and only by the grace of God, managed to remain afoot.

"If you are good, I may untie you later."

Why are you doing this to me her body screamed, but she had no voice with which to pose the question. She was his cousin, why would he apprehend and treat her thus?

She eyed him, using every essence of her being to remain steadfast. She couldn't ask her questions and he obviously wasn't going to volunteer the information, but God willing, she would not allow him to know the intimidation and worry that now seized her soul.

He smiled, but it did not bring her comfort. He looked like a snarling beast. "I could kill you, you know.

Everyone believes you are already dead. But I do not wish
the Rexley wrath on my head. Do as I say—sign away
your rights to Blackwell House and its holdings and I
shall let you live. Defy me and I will have no qualms
about slitting that delicate little throat of yours, Rexley
wrath or none. Do you comprehend me?"

She nodded emphatically and he closed the door,
leaving her standing alone in the middle of the room.
Desolation overflowed within her. It throbbed in her head,
ran through her veins, one with her very blood.

She heard a key turn in the lock, and only then did
she allow the waterfall to flow unheeded down her face.
She did not cry for long, however, before heated words
filtered underneath the door. She quieted her sobs.

"But, sir, you have never given *everyone* time off at
once. I thought perhaps—"

"You are not to think!" Aubury's too-familiar voice
abruptly cut off the unfamiliar one. "Do you understand?
Instructed all to get out and I meant you all to get out. If I
see you again before the three days are up I shall dismiss
you immediately and make sure you never find a position
in another household."

"Y-yes, Your Grace. I—I understand. Utmost."

Lark heard footsteps growing ever fainter and
realized they were going below stairs. Soon, all was silent
except for the muted tick of the mantle clock. Like cogs on
a wheel, Lark turned her head machine-like to the
fireplace. Twelve of the clock.

As if on queue, her stomach protested with a loud
groan. She was not hungry. It had only been a few hours
since she had taken her morning meal, but just the
possibility that she may never eat again caused the pangs
to intensify.

She turned around, scanning the room for means of
escape. The tent bed was large, the covering an ornate
Oriental pattern. No recollection of this room came to
mind. Besides, with her wrists bound, escape was
virtually impossible.

She slumped onto the edge of the bed and stared at
the cold, wooden floor beneath her feet. *Why did I not
listen to Jonathon?* The thought was like soured bubbles-
and-squeak implacably repeating to slap her squarely in

the face...And there was nothing worse than cabbage gone off.

She laid back on the bed and stared up at the canopy, her head still pounding. She raised her wrist-bound hands to her crown and felt a lump there the size of Wales. What had he done? Clobbered her with his cane?

Unsolicited, the tears began to flow once again.

Would she die on this bed, in this house, where once before her life had almost come to an end?

Chapter Twenty-Five

"Chauncy! Fetch my bag from the carriage." Jonathon slammed the front door.

Cyril emerged from the library. "There you are, brother."

"Yes, here am I. Is there a problem?" Jonathon took one look at Cyril's face and his own heart went stiff as a rock.

Cyril sported a blue-black eye and his bottom lip was split and swollen. His clothes were wrinkled and torn.

"Tell me nothing has happened to Lark." Jonathon's breathing went on hiatus as he waited for his brother's reply.

Cyril's mouth twitched. "Nothing has happened to Lark..."

Jonathon's lungs began to work.

"...that we know of."

Jonathon died inside. His breathing stopped and he felt light-headed and spongy-kneed. He found the nearest chair and lowered himself into it. "What happened?"

Cyril came to stand in front of him.

"I was duped," Cyril told him quietly. "I am sorry. I thought I could be of some assistance to your investigation. I knew you were skulking out things on Aubury. They lied and I...I turned to see..." His voice broke. "And she was gone."

"Blast! Blast! Blast!" Jonathon flew out of the chair. "I should not have left her alone."

"Nonsense. You didn't leave her alone. This is all my—"

Jonathon let out an angry snarl as he leapt from the chair, silencing his brother. He punished the floor with anxious steps. "Aubury's own sire believed he was responsible for his brother's death. I should have been more perceptive. If he harms Lark in any manner, I shall send him to hell myself!" He stormed out of the room, Cyril on his heels.

Harnessing horses to a carriage would have taken much too long. They almost did not wait for the stable boy to saddle the Bays. As they urged galloping horses onward there was no opportunity to speak. Jonathon could scarce believe the stories he had been told regarding the Aubury brothers, but he knew one thing: If Nigel Aubury had harmed Lark in any way, the man would greet the devil posthaste.

Horror gripped him at all the possibilities of Lark's fate his mind's eye displayed. He urged his horse to take on a faster pace, but the poor animal was already lathered in sweat.

Jonathon thought he understood the depth of true loss. When his father had tossed him out into the street, he thought then he had lost everything.

But he had been mistaken.

The full measure of loss was imbedded deep within the realm of the unknown. One lost so much more with the imagination than one ever could in reality.

His fear turned to anger, then attempted to manifest into resignation, but he refused to allow that.

Once they reached Blackwell House, he coaxed himself to remain calm. He could not walk up to a gentleman's door and outright accuse him of kidnapping or...or worse. Tact and guile would have to be his instruments.

But if he found out that Aubury had...his mind refused to give birth to the possibility of Lark's death.

The gate heralding the Blackwell property was ajar. Jonathon, an entire head in front of Cyril, slowed only enough to push it open without injuring his mount. Cyril barreled through seconds later.

The horses skidded to a halt as the reins yanked their heads backwards. Jonathon jumped from the stallion and Cyril grabbed his elbow. "We must be calm," Cyril said, his voice an urgent hiss.

"I know, but I'm finding it most difficult." Jonathon yanked his elbow from Cyril's grasp. "I fear I'm just going to remove Aubury's head from his body the minute I lay eyes on him."

"We cannot make accusations without proof. I wish to mangle the scalawag as much as you do, but the way to skin this cat is to make him lap the milk."

Jonathon paused, and took a calming breath. "I know," he managed to ground out, but he shook a gloved finger in Cyril's face. "But be forewarned. I do not know how long I can swallow my anger—and my tongue."

Cyril slapped his brother's finger away. "Let us get on with it." He walked up to the beveled door and pulled the cord. For quite some time they waited, the two of them, side by side on the steps of Blackwell House.

Rife with anticipation and worry, Jonathon raised his hand to the doorknocker and hammered the door with more force than was necessary.

He was on the brink of banging again when the door was finally unbolted. To his surprise, Aubury answered their herald personally. He wedged himself between the jamb and the barely open door, watery eyes peering out like stagnant ponds upon his face.

"Aubury, doing your own serving, these days?" Jonathon said, trying to unclench his teeth.

"Gave the servants the day off. Must keep them happy, you know, else they do you in while you sleep." He laughed, but it was a hollow sound that immediately put Jonathon at daggers drawn.

He stepped closer, and Cyril shot him a warning glance. Jonathon stepped back.

"Zounds, Rexley," Aubury said to Cyril, "looks as though you were hit by a horse." He sniffed.

"My brother is none of your concern," Jonathon bit out. Are you not going to invite us in?" He stepped up, giving Aubury no tangible option.

"Your hospitality is quite lacking," Cyril added.

Jonathon questioned Aubury with an arched eyebrow.

For several tense-filled moments, no one moved or spoke. Nigel seemed to weigh the possibilities then he thrust open the door. "Forgive me. I confess, caught me in the middle of reading a letter from a friend journeying through the Americas. Quite lost myself for a moment."

He led them into a room that Jonathon would have been hard-pressed to name, so intent was he on studying the inside of the house. The great room was a large expanse of highly decorated artwork and an ornate spiral staircase leading up to the first floor. It surprised Jonathon how much the house looked as it had before the fire. Aubury turned watery green eyes to them. "Care for a drink?"

"No," Jonathon ground out with barely-checked irritation.

"No *thank you*, Aubury," Cyril intoned. "We are here on urgent business. You don't mind answering a few inquiries?"

"N-no. Of course not." He moved away from them and came to stand with his back to the idle fireplace. He propped an elbow up on the mantle and almost knocked a vase into the lamp that sat next to it. Quickly he pulled away his arm and put a step's distance between himself and the fireplace.

Jonathon moved closer to Aubury, Cyril on his very heels. "You have not seen my betrothed? The one you met at Almack's some time ago?"

Aubury rang his hands together. "Why would I have seen her?" His attention darted from Jonathon to Cyril.

"We are unable to locate her, you see," Jonathon explained, quite successfully keeping his voice even and steady.

"That is a shame," Aubury put in. "But why do you think I would have knowledge of her whereabouts?" His gaze dropped to his hands and he immediately stilled the nervous movement of them. He looked to his visitors. Jonathon shot a quick glance to Cyril to see if he'd noticed Aubury's unease. He had, and Jonathon breathed a short sigh of relief that he and his brother were of like mind.

"We have no idea of her whereabouts. We are merely checking with everyone of acquaintance," Jonathon told him. His voice was still calm but his insides raged with the desire to shake the weasely duke into oblivion.

"Ah." Aubury shook his head and took a brave step towards them. He held out a hand, which now seemed suddenly relaxed. "I hope you have much success, however, I'm quite positive I shouldn't know where she is." He forced out a laugh. "Perhaps you scared the young gel away."

"You fubsy, bracket-faced bouncer. You know perfectly well that Lark is a Blackwell. What have you done with her? Tell us now before I put my hands around your blubbery neck and squeeze the worthless life out of you." Jonathon shook his fist at Aubury, but Cyril successfully maneuvered past Jonathon.

Aubury attempted a shocked countenance. "A Blackwell, you say? Why, that would make the lovely angel a cousin of mine own." A dramatic hand came to his chest, and he focused his eyes on Jonathon. "Do let me know when you find her. How delightful that I should have kin after the tragic passing of my own brother."

The fraying string that had held Jonathon's temper together broke loose completely. With lightening reflexes, he shoved Cyril out of the way, balled his fist, and chopped Aubury right on the nose.

Flesh kissed flesh with a shattering sound and Aubury's body flew backwards.

"Good show!" Cyril called.

Aubury scrambled to balance, dabbing his nose with the back of his hand. Blood stained his skin. He lunged at Jonathon.

Jonathon caught him and flung him back again. Aubury's arms flailed and smacked the marble mantle with a crunch that could only mean broken bones.

A photograph toppled to the floor. The crash of broken glass echoed through the room. The oil lamp wobbled then tumbled to the marble hearth, shattering instantly.

Flame ignited the nearby rug and Aubury scampered away from the heat and collapsed, still not a safe distance from the fire.

For a moment, Jonathon and Cyril stood transfixed. Then Jonathon turned and fled the room. "Take care of him. I must look for Lark." The fire spread across the floor, touched a drapery hem, and skittered up the wall.

"She may not be here," Cyril yelled. "We must get out before the..." his voice trailed off. "...fire spreads."

Jonathon glanced back and witnessed as Cyril quickly closed the distance between himself and Lark's cousin. As he bent to pick up the unconscious body, life sprang from Aubury. With a push born of sheer

181

adrenaline, Aubury knocked Cyril to the ground.

Scrambling from atop Cyril's startled, prone body, Aubury dashed out of the room and up the stairs.

Cyril could take care of himself; Jonathon had to find Lark.

****

She thought it was a dream—a terrible nightmare. Groggily, she opened her eyes and tried to focus on something—anything. The pungent odor of smoke grabbed her nostrils. Fear gripped her as once again she was five years old...

She could feel the coolness of the wooden step seeping through her cotton nightdress, chilling the soles of her bare feet. Her parents' voices mingled with that of Lady Somerset's—Auntie May—They did not sound at all happy. Auntie May sounded as if she were crying.

Lark slid her bottom down another step and peered through the railings of the banister, trying to hear, trying to discover why her parents had sent her to her bedchamber so soon after Auntie May arrived.

"I did a terrible thing." That was Auntie May's voice, cracking through the sobs. "I did not have a mind to do otherwise. When Peter told me..."

Lark did not hear any more of what Auntie May had to say. Her attention was pulled away by a muffled noise coming from the kitchen.

Sadie was still up. Perhaps she could be persuaded to give Lark a biscuit. Quite like a burglar, she thought with a tiny smile, she inched her way down the stairs. She could smell smoke already. Sadie must be fixing something good.

Excitement bubbled in her tummy. Lark had completely forgotten about her parents and Lady Somerset. Sadie was going to be surprised to see her, but the old cook would be convinced to give her a taste of whatever it was she was preparing.

Lark made it to the bottom of the stairs and tiptoed with exaggerated steps across the open room towards the kitchen. She slid open the kitchen door and froze.

"Lark Blackwell!"

Chapter Twenty-Six

"Lark!" The sound of her name brought her mind reeling to the present. Her eyes popped open and she found herself still flat on her back on the bed. She rolled to one side and inched her way to a sitting position. Her mind whirled. What was happening?

Smoke seeped into the room from underneath the door and Lark knew an unparalleled terror. Tears sprang to her eyes. She slid to the floor and used her elbows to drag herself under the bed.

No. No. This was not a good place to be.

She began to inch her way back out but a rattling at the door stopped her. Someone was trying to get in.

Aubury.

Inside she screamed. She retreated further under the bed and cowered out of sight. The door rattled more fiercely.

"Lark!"

Jonathon's voice was hoarse from yelling, and even he didn't see the logic in it. If Lark were here, even if she could hear him, she would not be able to cry out. He rattled the door again. It was definitely locked.

Smoke pooled around his ankles like fog rolling over the glen. Time was expiring quickly. He hoped Cyril had gotten out of the house and to safety.

He backed across the hall to the opposite wall and took a running start at forcing open the door. His shoulder connected hard as he rammed into the wood. Pain shot down his arm.

The door did not give way.

Urgency welled inside him as he readied for another attempt. The pain in his arm did not subside. He ignored it. If Lark were in there, nothing would stop him from retrieving her.

With his uninjured arm, he reached up and wiped

the smoke-driven tears away from his eyes. The smoke thickened. His lungs filled with it. With every breath, they burned as much as his eyes stung.

He charged the door a second time. The wood around the latch splintered and gave way. With a fierce thrust, he shoved open the door. He swiped at his eyes again. He could barely see through the gray haze, and then he heard scraping and scratching.

"Lark? Lark!" He waved away the smoke to no avail and, as he staggered into the room, he was hit with such force—by a projectile so large—he was knocked back into the corridor and onto the floor.

His head bounced off the hard wood and for a moment floating sparks danced before his eyes. He tried to focus and scramble out from underneath whatever had captured him.

And then he seized a glimpse.

"Lark."

Happiness flowed over him, and he momentarily forgot the impeding peril. Forgetting himself, he held her captive and bathed her face in a million kisses.

"We must hurry," he said, when he finally was of his mind again. As he rolled her off him, he noticed her bound wrists. "Damnation!" Hurriedly, he began to work the knots in the rope.

A sharp, cutting pain shot down his arm from his shoulder. He sucked in a smoke-filled breath then coughed out the lungful of contaminated oxygen.

"Jonathon." Cyril's voice rang out.

"Damnation," Jonathon bit out again. "Here, Cyril." He did not wait to see if his brother found his way before continuing to free Lark. He unbound her wrists, and she threw her arms around his neck. "I love you, too, my dear, but we must hurry." He reached up and untangled himself from her, ignoring the searing pain in his shoulder.

Cyril's image sliced through the smoke as Jonathon got to his feet. "Thank God you found her." Cyril choked and sputtered.

"What the devil are you doing in here? I told you to get out."

"I suppose now you are going to stand here amid the

smoke and lecture me on not following your direction? Do you know there were actual flames following me up these stairs?"

Lark began to cough uncontrollably, and both men turned their attention to her. Jonathon commenced to pull her to her feet when a shadow came through the smoke from the opposite direction. Confusion ruled him for a lapsed moment as he tried to reason how someone could have gotten past them on the stairs.

An arm grabbed at Lark. Jonathon's instinct blotted out reason. He jerked Lark up, and in one thrust, threw her behind him into Cyril's arms. "Get her out. *Quickly*."

He spun back around to greet the assailant and found himself knocked to the floor.

Lark struggled to free herself of Cyril's grasp. She was not leaving Jonathon behind. Flames rose from the ground floor. A section of the banister gave way.

"Stop it. We must get out," Cyril yelled, but she did not take heed.

She wrenched her arm free and began to make her way back to Jonathon. She ignored the treacherous heat of the fire and the way her skirts clung to her sweating body. Onward she moved, one purpose in mind only.

She strained to see through the haze of smoke. Jonathon was struggling to his feet.

Another part of the banister gave way, the stairs quickly turning to ash below them.

A figure lunged at Jonathon from behind.

"Jonathon!"

It was Lark's first and last word. The stairs collapsed underneath her and she fell to the smoldering floor below.

Chapter Twenty-Seven

Jonathon heard Lark's warning. It was a bittersweet sound. He catapulted forward and out of the way. His assailant collapsed on the landing face down. Jonathon spun around.

Aubury.

Jonathon pounced and pinned the man, rolled him over, and smashed him in the face with a balled angry fist.

Aubury's head lolled to one side. He shook it off and grabbed Jonathon around the neck.

The landing creaked beneath their weight. Flames rose to the ceiling from where the banister once had been sturdy and strong.

Linked together as one, they struggled, rolling to the wall, then to the burning edge of the stairs.

Embers popped all around but neither of them seemed to notice. Aubury, once again on top, squeezed Jonathon's neck. He struggled for air.

Wood cracked and splintered. A beam fell.

Jonathon let out a guttural growl as he expelled all his energy to get out of the way.

It didn't work. Jonathon and Aubury were trapped.

****

She was on fire. Through the smoky haze, she could see Cyril easing up off the floor, his face twisted as if it hurt to move. He rolled onto his knees. His eyes met hers and he cut through the smoke quickly.

Cyril knelt over her frantically beating her skirts with his coat. She shrieked and rolled out of the way, completely out of her mind.

Jonathon.

Instinct and adrenaline gave her an edge over Cyril. She scampered to her feet, the fire in her skirts out now. He lunged and knocked her to the floor.

She struggled to gain freedom but his weight was much too much for her to overcome.

He grappled to gain footing without allowing her to escape.

She twisted, inching her way free.

Her efforts were to no avail.

Cyril picked her up and threw her over his shoulder like a baby's doll. She beat on his back with her fists.

He ignored her and made haste towards the exit.

She continued her tirade, flailing her legs and screaming. Still he ignored her.

Once free from the inferno, he plopped her onto the earth. "What the devil did you think you were doing in there? Did you wish to die?"

She scrambled off the ground. Screaming at him, she lunged forward. He caught her wrists, effectively ceasing her pummeling of his chest. She tried to speak but her throat felt like a peeled potato.

He spun her around easily and held her stationary against his chest. "Do you swear to calm yourself if I set you free?"

She struggled more. He tightened his grip. "Swear it!"

She nodded. He eased his grasp and she tried to bolt.

"Widgeon!" He held her captive. "Be sensible! Do you want to die?" He turned her to face him once again. "Calm yourself," he coaxed, keeping his voice low and even.

Lark nodded. Warily this time he eased his grasp. She remained steadfast, and he freed her completely.

She collapsed to the grassy earth. Heat rose on her face in time to the flame-light that flashed from the burning house. Tears soaked her cheeks. She swiped them away and streaks of black soot came off on her glove. Cyril turned to look at the collapsing house then fell to the ground at her side.

Fire illuminated the sky like day. Lark stared at the house. One side crumbled, crackled, and fell to the earth as a mass of flaming embers, and once again, Lark was five years old...

Rebekka huddled over her, trying to cover her face, but Lark did not want to be protected. She wanted Mama. She wanted Papa. She had tried to run back into the house, to find them, to save them, but Rebekka would not allow it.

Rebekka was mean. Rebekka was a turncoat.

The fire brigade was on the way. The bells clanged in the distance. Maybe one of them would listen to her—even if she were only a child.

And then she saw her mama. She tried to break free of Rebekka's hold.

"Mama," she cried, but Rebekka kept her captive.

"I am sorry about your mama," Rebekka said, drawing Lark's attention away from the figure of her mama coming forth from the flames.

Lark shook her head. Rebekka did not understand. She raised a tiny hand and pointed towards the house. "Mam—"

Her mama was gone.

And then, from out of nowhere Lord Peter appeared. Fear seized Lark's throat. She tried to escape Rebekka's grasp but Rebekka held her captive. She began to cry.

"Thank heavens you are safe," Lord Peter had said as he took her into his arms. She squirmed in his arms and he tightened his grip. It hurt.

"Come quickly," he told Rebekka. "We must leave at once."

"But, my lord, the fire brigade will be here any minute," Rebekka said.

"Yes, but you do not understand. It is imperative we leave at once. For Lark's well-being."

"Very well." Rebekka followed him into the forestry on the other side of the clearing and they escaped.

Sobs racked Lark's body as past and present collided. She had lost everything twelve years ago—much more even than she had remembered until this very night—and now, she had lost Jonathon, too.

A small explosion brought her head jolting up. More windows burst from the building. Another section collapsed.

She wailed. "Jonathon!" The name sprung forth from her raw throat rent with anguish. Cyril looked at her.

Lark flung herself at him, and he cradled her in his arms while she cried like a tot.

She didn't know how long she cried, but suddenly her

eyes were dry. Inside she was still empty, but her tears were spent and gone. She sat up, pulling herself free from Cyril's arms and looked at him through swollen, red-rimmed eyes.

"I know," he said softly.

Devoid of emotion, now, she turned to look at the inferno that was once her home—a home she had wiped from memory. Only one section remained in tact. Smoke and flames billowed from it mercilessly. She wiped away a tendril of hair that had fallen into her face.

And the hallucination began.

She tried to reason away the mirage, tried to tell herself to be sensible and calm. She was no longer a child fooled by images only her mind wished to create. She blinked and shook her head, but the image refused to vanish.

Hope soared.

Sensibility vanquished it.

Freshly pooled tears stung the backs of her eyes. She was losing sanity.

"Jonathon!" Cyril's loud, booming voice startled her. Her head turned to him but he was already sprinting towards her mirage.

Joy soared within her chest. It was really Jonathon, dragging something—someone.

Another small explosion sparked within the inferno and the remainder of the house fell in a burning heap. Jonathon fell to the ground.

Lark bolted to her feet and ran to his fallen body. Behind him lay Nigel Aubury muttering something about no fire protection. Her cousin. Jonathon still had a grip on Aubury's foot.

She fell at Jonathon's side, rubbed her hand along his face. His breathing was labored, and she feared that she might lose him after all.

"That is it for Aubury," Cyril said, not even the slightest remorse apparent in his voice.

Lark turned to see her cousin's charred and lifeless form. She could not conjure any sorrow.

"Lark," Jonathon croaked. Her head came back to him immediately.

And then he went limp.

189

Chapter Twenty-Eight

Sunlight streamed in the hospital window, and Lark took it upon herself to draw the curtain. Jonathon opened his eyes and smiled at her.

"You look a mess," she signed. His face was bandaged, as was his right hand. His left arm was bent at the elbow and secured; his shoulder had been fractured.

"Speak to me." His voice was raspy, stripped raw from smoke inhalation.

She shook her head. "I cannot," she said with her hands.

"You can. I heard you." He grinned at her through the bandages. "Jolly good thing, too. You saved me from being clobbered a good one." He began to cough.

She gently touched his arm. "Do not speak." She spoke the words slowly, quietly and a smile came across Jonathon's lips that warmed her heart.

The Sister came down the ward corridor to Jonathon's bed. "Ready to unmask, Lord Somerset?" She asked cheerfully.

Jonathon nodded.

Sister turned to Lark. "I must—"

Cyril came bursting in with his cousin, Marie. "Do say we're not late," Cyril boomed. "It's Marie's fault. She absolutely would not leave without *those* gloves." He pointed to the wretched things as if they were a disease.

"They match my dress exactly," Marie explained. "Heavens, I had to look the utmost for the unveiling of my best cousin." She touched a hand to her expanding stomach. "Especially since I am in this hideously swelled state." They came to stand beside Lark.

Cyril clutched his chest. "You wound me, Cousin. That *I* should not be your favorite." He shrugged it off. "Ah well, you always did have questionable taste."

Marie hit him with her reticule and the ward Sister

gasped.

"Please. I am going to have to ask you all to take your leave. We must unbandage and balm Lord Somerset. It is not a welcome sight, I assure you."

"What say you, brother? May we stay and have a look."

"I'm not budging one bit," Lark signed.

"What was that?" Cyril asked.

"She said she's not moving," Rebekka said, coming up from behind them. She forced her way between Cyril and Marie and spoke to Lark. "And I have told you, you must begin to speak, else you will surely forget how."

"Yes, Rebekka," Lark said. Her voice may be new to her, but sarcasm certainly was not. Rebekka scoffed and faced off with the ward Sister. "We are all staying, so you might as well proceed with haste."

Cyril chuckled. "Here, here," he said. He leaned to Marie. "Remind me of this next time I am hiring house staff. I think I shall hire only gentlemen from now on," he whispered.

The doctor arrived and Sister relayed that he was evidently going to have an audience this morning. He looked at the entourage and shook his head. "If any of you females has an attack of the vapors, I shall let you fall to the floor and leave you to your own devices." He shooed them away from the bed. "Now, make room. Make room."

****

"Cyril mentioned you might have memories of the first fire?" Jonathon leaned back against the gazebo. It had been hence six weeks since he was released from hospital. His skin was still red and chaffed from the exposure to the fire, but the doctor said he would recover fully. There would always be scars on his arm, though.

Lark bit into a biscuit. She shook her head. "I didn't tell him that." Speaking with her mouth was becoming a welcome habit.

"Look, Aubury may have breathed his last, but we still must be positive there is no further danger to you."

She avoided his eyes. "There is no danger. I am positive."

He leaned forward and covered her hand as it rested on the seat beside her. "I wish to be positive, also."

191

She raised her eyes to his. "Can you not just forget? We have a wedding to prepare. 'Tis a happy time." She looked out at their surroundings. "The day is beautiful. The birds are our orchestra, and we have plans for the theater this eve. Let us not spoil it with things of no consequence." She closed her eyes and prayed he would dismiss the subject post-haste. What she had remembered was better remained forgotten.

He uncrossed his legs and stood up. She lifted her head to meet his gaze. "I almost forgot," he said cheerfully. He opened his coat and reached into his vest pocket.

"This is for you, my dearest." He bent and handed her a small black velvet box.

Slowly, she took it in her own hands. With trembling fingers, she unhinged the jewelry case to unveil the most delicate, most beautiful, most intricately sculpted angel brooch.

She sucked in her breath. "Jonathon it is lovely." She stood and kissed his cheek. "I shall cherish it always. Do pin it on me."

He took the brooch and pinned it to the bodice of her morning dress. Looking into her eyes, he held her captive. "Do you know why I chose this for you?"

She shook her head, unable to speak.

"Because the moment I discovered it I thought of you. Of your innocence. Of your beauty. You are an angel, my love. *My* angel, and no longer the Somerset Ghost." He nudged her chin with the side of his hand. "And angels do not lie." He pleaded with her. "Tell me what you remember."

She slumped down onto the seat. "You are a cad!" she told him.

"I know. But I do so love you and want you always to be safe." He sat beside her and took both of her hands in his. "You do not know the anguish I endured when I returned home to find you gone. Business will take me away from time to time. I have to know you are safe."

"But I am," she told him. "Please don't make me tell you. Please, *please* don't make me tell you. It is past and best forgotten." She searched his face and saw the uncertainty existing there. He would never be content;

she could see it in his eyes. She sighed. "All right."

He smiled but she knew he would not smile for long.

She pulled free of him and stood up. The cool breeze chilled her hands where they had been warmed by Jonathon's touch. She hoped his heart would not be thusly chilled by her words.

She circled the gazebo, searching her mind for the proper place to begin. When finally she had some semblance of a story in her mind, she spoke. "I bore witness to who set the fire. But I do not know his motive. I think—"

"Aubury, yes I know." Jonathon cut her off.

"No," Lark said, so softly the word was almost carried away on the breeze.

"Well, not *Nigel* Aubury, but rather his brother," Jonathon explained. "What I need to know is can you remember anything that might put someone else in the picture, someone still—"

Lark shook her head. He was making this best difficult. "It was neither of my cousins," she said. She ignored Jonathon's frown of confusion.

Tears sprung to her eyes as she contemplated her next words. She held them back a time.

"Lord Peter." Her voice cracked with a sob, and she cleared her throat to disguise it.

Jonathon sat there, staring, frozen. For several moments, the tension rose between them. "What?" He asked finally. "You must be mistaken. He saved you."

She found the seat and lowered her body, her weight suddenly too heavy for her legs to bear. She shook her head and began to tell him all she could remember. "...He was leaving through the kitchen when Rebekka startled me. The fire spread quickly. I didn't realize what was happening." She looked at him with torment in her eyes. "He lit the curtain with a matchstick on his way out. The table was already aflame."

"But how did you escape if you were so close to the fire." She could see the disbelief in his eyes as he struggled to comprehend her words.

"Rebekka startled me. I was supposed to be in my bed. She shuttled me upstairs silencing my pleas for her to listen. Then the flames caught up with us. It happened so quickly. She took me down the back stairs, through the secret passageway."

"That was how Aubury got above stairs without having to pass us." Jonathon said absently.

"I suppose so." Lark studied her hands. They were sore from being wrung together. "I am sorry, Jonathon."

He studied her face. "That still does not explain why. Why would my father deliberately kill his best friend? His own wife? He adored my mother; he practically went insane without her."

Lark sighed heavily. She had known the moment she had begun that she would have to reveal everything. "Come," she said.

As she led Jonathon to her chambers, apprehension imprisoned him. He did not wish to know whatever she had to divulge, yet if he didn't let her reveal it, he would never know another day's peace.

She ordered Rebekka out with no apparent compunction, which set alarm bells ringing inside Jonathon immediately. Lark always showed Rebekka the utmost respect.

Rebekka seemed no worse for her curt dismissal as she curled her lips at Lord Somerset on her way out.

"Do sit," Lark told him as she went to her wardrobe, turned the key, and opened the door. She crouched to the floor, and the rustling of her skirts was amplified to his heightened senses.

His gaze moved mechanically to the chairs in front of the idle fireplace, but he could not sit. His heart pounded within his chest, his pulse registering in his ears. Perspiration dotted his brow.

She retrieved something from the wardrobe, rose to her full height, and turned to face him. She was holding a leather-backed book. "While you were in hospital, I searched for this." She offered it to him. His arm extended itself of its own accord and took it from her.

She crossed in front of him and took a seat. "I knew Lord Peter must keep one somewhere, for it was he who encouraged me to do the same."

Jonathon opened the cover. *Journal of Peter Rexley, Lord Somerset* was written in his father's bold hand.

"Turn to page twenty," she instructed him.

The crinkling of the paper boomed with his growing trepidation as he turned the pages.

Page twenty.

...I know not how she found out, but when she confronted me, I did not have the heart to continue the lies. She even accused me of fathering Lark because of the resemblance in our birth blemishes. Mere coincidence. I told her as much and confessed all regarding Geoffry so there could be complete and utter truth between us once again. It did no good. I considered myself an utter rake, but little did I know that she, my only love, was a dolly-mop. And with my own best friend. How could she—how could Darin—be so unfaithful to me? They shall not bring shame to this household again. She goes to him now, I am positive of it, but it shall be the last time they make a fool of me...

Jonathon turned the page. *Oh, what have I done? Wrath. Forgive me. The child lives but does not speak. I cannot bring myself this day to...I cannot utter the word. I must but keep her hidden. If the world believes she is perished, too, then I am safe. Her maid is but convinced of my charm, and my sons are men and gone....*Jonathon raised his face to Lark's. Tears blurred his vision but he would never allow them to fall.

"But why? It makes not an ounce of sense. If you were a threat to him, why did he not just..."

She lifted her shoulders. "He was not a murderer, Jonathon. He cared for me. After everything, I believe still that he cared for me. He acted in anger and hurt, I am sure. Once he had regained himself, he could not kill an innocent child in cold blood."

She dropped her gaze and sniffed back tears. Jonathon's heart twisted. "Please don't cry, Lark. It will be my undoing."

"And it was *untrue.*" The word ripped from her as she buried her face in her hands.

"What?"

She raised her eyes to his face. "She lied to him. I heard her telling Mama and Papa. She said, 'I did a terrible thing...I lied when I discovered he strayed, had a son...I made up tales of an affair with Darin.' I did not comprehend of what she spoke. I thought she had gone on an outing of some kind. And then I paid no heed. I smelled something cook...ing." Her voice trailed off. She stared at Jonathon for extended moments. "Read the last page, his final entry."

Jonathon slowly flipped the pages with one finger. *I cannot give Lark back what I have so wrongfully taken but I may give her back a life. It will take more lies, but I am adept at them now. Jonathon will not doubt me. He is the utmost best son, sticking by me when Cyril and the rest think I am unworthy. He will take care of her and I shall be content.*

Jonathon slammed the book closed and hurled it across the room. Lark started and stared at the heap of torn pages. "A murderer and a scoundrel! A murder and a scoundrel. What a man was my father." He stormed from the room.

Lark let him go. Six weeks ago, when she had finally found the hidden journal, she had felt exactly the same.

Chapter Twenty-Nine

Lark hid behind the potted palm in the vestibule of St. Rita's. She felt quite overcome by the throng of people filling the pews of the medium-sized church. She glanced upward to the stained glass window. Jesus Christ looked down on her with benevolence and love shining in his amber, sun-filled eyes. Lark could not imagine being happier than she was at this moment.

"She is a wonderful gel." Aunt Harriet's voice pulled Lark's attention.

The woman she had addressed nodded an acceptance, and Lark smiled. Lady Wescotte was certainly on her best behavior this afternoon. She had even smiled at Geoffry—Something Lark would have never believed after the dreadful way the lady had treated him in the library so many months ago. Even Jonathon had mentioned her softened demeanor.

"Whatever happened with her deficiency?" a sour-faced old bat in a green empire dress dared to ask, her ample bosom resting on the back of a pew as she leaned over.

"If you ask me, Lark never had a deficiency," Marie spoke up, evidently with no care that she drew the attention of half the crowd. "Lark has always been the utmost pattern-card of charity and goodness." She looked pointedly to the bat-woman. "Some would do well to learn manners from the likes of Lark."

The woman grumbled something Lark could not hear. A smile came to Lark's lips as she stifled a giggle.

"Eavesdropping again, my dear Miss Lark?"

Lark spun to see Jonathon behind her. "Is it not bad luck for the bride to see the groom before the wedding?"

"So it is," intoned Cyril, bringing up the rear.

"As we have done nothing thus far the way it is supposed to be done, I don't think we have to worry about

197

bad luck. We are quite fortunate."

"I'll toast to that!" Cyril quipped.

"You'll toast to anything," Jonathon told him.

Cyril shrugged. "Nothing wrong with being festive."

Lark smiled, seeing only Jonathon. "I am the most fortunate, my lord. The luckiest lady in the world."

"Oh, posh! I must take my leave before you two melt completely to mush right here on the carpet." Cyril huffed, and then walked off.

Jonathon watched his brother depart then turned back to his bride. He rested his hands delicately upon her shoulders. "I am much luckier than you, my dear. You are beyond compare. To think I might never have found you had I been left to my own devises."

"I am so glad Lord Peter loved me enough to enjoin me to you. I have loved you forever."

He pulled her close and placed a gentle kiss on her lips.

Lark's pulse quickened with the warm tenderness of Jonathon's lips on hers. Her eyes fluttered closed, and she brought her hands up to cradle his head. Happiness and contentment became tangible; she felt more complete than she ever had in the past.

Moments later, the spell was broken as Cyril interrupted by clearing his throat. "Time to go, Romeo," he said, tapping Jonathon on the shoulder.

Lark turned her attention to the finely dressed man behind Cyril. "You look quite fabulous, Chauncy," she said.

"I must agree," opined Jonathon sincerely.

Lark had never known Chauncy to blush before, and the boyish reaction touched her heart. "I am so grateful that you would agree to escort me down the aisle," she told him.

Chauncy bowed. "It is highly unusual, my lady, but I am thoroughly honored."

"As Jon pointed out, everything about these two is highly unusual. Come on, brother, let us get you in the right place. Everyone awaits." Cyril tugged on Jonathon's arm and Lord Somerset obediently followed.

Standing on the threshold of the sanctuary Jonathon watched Lark glide down the aisle with swanlike grace, and he realized fully this was truly the best day of his life. It had taken weeks for him to come to terms with the past. The man he knew as his father had seemed never to exist. It rent his heart, but he had finally come to realize that this happiest moment would not exist without being moulded by the past.

"He loved me enough to enjoin me with you." Lark's earlier words came back to him. She had the right of it. His father had been more flawed than Jonathon could ever have imagined, but in the end Peter Rexley had been utmost remorseful and diligent in setting things aright.

As the organ music swelled in his ears, the only person who filled his vision was Lark Blackwell. Peter Rexley and all that man's sordid secrets were dead and gone. Now, nothing existed except a bright and happy life with his resurrected lady wife.

Author's Note

Although deaf-mutes were considered uneducable, in the mid 18th century, Charles-Michel, abbé de Epée (1712-89) developed a system of communication that involved spelling out words with a manual alphabet and expressing whole concepts with simple signs. His early system developed into French Sign Language (FSL), which is still used in France today.

In the early 19th century, Epée's successor, abbé Roch-Ambroise Sicard, taught FSL to a young Yale graduate named Thomas Gallaudet. In 1816, Gallaudet brought the system to the United States.

American Sign Language (ASL) is the fourth most commonly used language in the USA and is used by more than 500,000 deaf people in North America.

****

I hope you enjoyed The Resurrection of Lady Somerset. I welcome your comments, so please visit me on the web at http://www.inicola.net.

Blessings,
Nicola Beaumont

3 1524 00479 6183

Printed in the United States
90289LV00005B/5/A